Contents

Prologue

Bruno sighed as he watched Joey absently pacing again. The young smith had done it several times a day over the past week. At first, Bruno had mistaken it for worry of John returning. The man was a traitor and a killer, among other, more monstrous things, and Joey had seen firsthand what he could do. But as the week went on, it was clear this was a different kind of anxiety.

At the point that Bruno saw the tool in his hand, he knew it was time to say something. He removed his gloves, walked over, and set a hand on Joey's shoulder. The young man nearly touched the rafters with how high he jumped. Bruno eased, "Now, I may be pulling at straws here, but you seem a little high strung."

"Remember to pick the kids up from school tomorrow," was the only reply as Joey began to pace again. Bruno frowned. It was the third time he'd been reminded by the wreck in front of him. Bruno suggested, "Why don't we step outside?"

"I'm fine, really-"

"Joey." The younger finally stopped and ran his fingers through dark blonde hair. But after a moment, he nodded and headed for the front door. Bruno followed, only to have Andrew catch his arm, warning, "You know-"

1

"I know," Bruno cut off quietly, patting his friend on the back. Joey's hand fidgeted as Bruno strode out to meet him, fingers playing some tune in his head. The elder closed the door behind him and cautiously asked, "What's going on?"

Though it took a few seconds for an answer, Joey finally gave, "It's been almost a year. He hasn't done anything in almost year, Bruno, the kids-"

"The kids will be fine. I'll-" Bruno detected the slight sound of a bush rustling, too much for an animal in the area. Someone was watching. "-I'll pick them up tomorrow. And if for some reason I can't, then you can do it. Give yourself some security-"

"They're in danger," he worried. Bruno stared at the man as he started to retreat back into his head. That is, until he inquired, "How do you do it? How are you so calm? How, under all the pressure of him attacking them, are you not worried?"

Bruno crossed his arms, sensing some of the tension in his own joints. "I am worried. I know my brother, and it only makes it worse, knowing what he is capable of. But…"

He shrugged, "…someone has to be calm. If that's me, then so be it."

They both stood there, completely silent. Bruno heard that rustle again, and fought to not acknowledge it. Joey's nerves were running. If he knew how right he was about the danger, he might crack. The younger's hand was still fidgeting, though at a slower pace. Bruno only then realized the night sky had long since appeared. It was hard for him to differentiate between day and night, sometimes.

The rustle was close enough now that Bruno caught Joey's brow crease. Bruno quickly insisted, "Get some sleep. You've been stressed the whole week. You need to let your body rest."

"I doubt the gears in my head will shut down," Joey muttered, Bruno silently cursing him for not getting inside immediately. Just as he started to protest, an object zipped out from the underbrush nearby, sticking Joey in the neck. He pulled out a dart and stared at it a second before fainting. Bruno didn't quite expect to be tackled by an unconscious body, but felt his feet go out from under him before anything could be done about it. Someone was quick to run out and point a gun at him, a second dart hitting Bruno in the side of the chest. Though he struggled to stay conscious, the last thing Bruno saw was the figure leaning down and picking up Joey's wrist.

Reason to Worry

1

I stuffed my folder into my bag as fast as humanly possible when the final bell rang. Not only was it finally summer, but next year, I would officially be a high schooler. I hooted and hollered with the other eighth graders as some made their ways to the bus lot, while others headed for parking lot pick up. I, on the other hand, hurried toward the back gate so I could hop it and get into the woods to meet the blacksmiths for practice. Over the past year, I'd gotten a lot better in my sparring. And now that I could actually win sometimes, practice had gotten really fun.

"Jamaica! Hey, Jamaica! Wait up!" Anna yelled over the sea of students, elbowing her way through to me. The mass of bodies finally spread out a bit more, so she was able to pull me over to the side wall. We were both laughing in excitement as she told me, "I've got a dentist appointment today, so I'm gonna be late to training."

"Okay, that's cool," I waved off, "I'll tell Bruno-"

"Jamaica!" My cousin K.C. called. She had already made it to the woods, but was pushing her way back upstream to us. She scoffed at some kid's complaint and dramatically dove to us, hands smacking against the wall to catch her. Panting, she informed, "Hi, Anna. Jamaica, we've gotta go. Joey said to grab Mark, too."

The panic in her eyes was obvious. I turned to my best friend and excused, "We'll catch you up when you get to practice."

Before I could see her reaction, my cousin and I were swimming through the crowd. I shouted over the chatting, "Where's Mark?"

"Over by the buses! He's with friends!" she replied. The bus lot wasn't anywhere near the forest side of campus, what was he doing there?

Lo and behold, there he was giggling and goofing off with his buddies. I broke from the crowd and called, "Mark!"

Mark, my other cousin, looked over, smiled, waved, and went back to his group. I put my head in one hand and groaned. K.C. made her way back to my side, huffing, "Good luck getting him away from them. You'd think they were glued together."

"We'll see," I grumbled. I marched up to him, chiding, "Mark, c'mon, we've gotta go-"

"Just hold on a minute, J. So, he's managed to get himself halfway through the ceiling, right-?"

"Mark, *now*," I pressed through gritted teeth, trying to get the message across to him that something was wrong. He noticed, smile dropping as he briefly licked his lips. Mark apologized, "Sorry, guys, I gotta go."

"Aw, c'mon, you didn't finish the story-"

"I'll finish it later, but I have to go." He walked past me, not seeing the stink eyes coming my way. I hurried after him, and soon as I fell into step, he asked, "Do you know what's going on?"

"No. But K.C. is freaking out, and that's never good." K.C. joined up with us a moment later and we made our way to the

5

back-gate perimeter, climbing up and over. I looked up the hill at a whistle to see Joey almost entirely hidden in the bushes. We hiked up to him, and soon found two other blondes waiting.

"Trace? Jamie?" K.C.'s brow knit, "I thought you guys still had another half hour of remedial."

"We did," Jamie agreed, letting Trace add, "We snuck out."

"You spied on me again?" I indignantly scowled, "Trace!"

My boyfriend, Trace, and his little sister, Jamie, had come back into the modern world with a surprising welcome, the story of a family gone missing eight years before hitting headlines. Their father was able to adjust incredibly fast, getting back on his feet in just a few months and renting a small apartment with a little help from the community's donations. Trace and Jamie had been placed in remedial classes to catch up on all the schooling they had missed. Both soaked up the information like sponges for the most part, Trace already going through the essentials of a fourth-grade syllabus, and Jamie right behind him, just starting on a third. They would be introduced into public school when they were close enough to the learning curve.

And they were slowly ruining their chances by sneaking out of class to come spy on me. Trace reminded, "You are a target."

"So are you!" I retorted, "So are Mark and K.C., but you don't spy on them!"

"And thank god he doesn't," K.C. mumbled, making me shoot her an annoyed look. Trace argued, "Let me rephrase that- you're the main target!"

"Main target or not, I don't need you spying on me! You should be catching up on your school courses, you're so close-!"

"Hardly," he denied, to which I swiftly cut back in, "Then you should be working to *get* close-!"

Joey cleared his throat.

We'll settle this later.

6

Trace's ears shifted back like a dog's as he swallowed. Jamie poked Joey's shoulder, pestering, "*Now* will you tell us why Bruno didn't pick them up today?"

The thought hit me, and I wondered, "Yeah, where is Bruno?"

Joey took a deep breath before explaining, "We were outside the workshop last night, he was trying to talk me down from my nerves. All I remember was a dart hit my neck, and I passed out. When I woke up this morning, Bruno was nowhere to be seen, and I now I have this on my wrist."

He held up his right arm to present a watch like device with a stomach sinking familiarity. My first reaction was to try and soothe Trace, but he started mumbling, "Get it off him. Get it off him, Jamaica, it hurts, get it off him. Get it off him! Get it off-!"

Mark pushed him back as his voice rose, the firebender's protective instinct flaring. A thin whip of water suddenly formed, giving them both a jab in the nose to break the tension between them. K.C. cried, "Knock it off! She can remove it when we get back to the workshop, okay?"

The boys complied, hands over the middle of their faces. As we made our way deeper into the woods, I fell back to Trace, walking behind everyone else. He eyed the device on Joey warily, seemingly ready to rip it off himself at any moment. To distract him, I asked, "So…how's the family doing? Rehabilitation, I mean."

Still watching, he replied, "The psychologist says Jamie still has high levels of- hypervigilance. I think she said it basically just means Jamie has trust issues. No one can get Mom to be verbal. I don't really think she needs to be, and the people helping her aren't patient enough to learn sign language."

He scowled at this, but kept going, "The psychologist is most worried about Dad. He hasn't shown any signs of really being affected by what happened. I mean, he's worn out by it, and the

7

subject is sensitive, but…it's like he treats it as a distant memory. Like it happened a long time ago."

His frown brought out my sympathy, but I pushed, "And what about you?"

He faked a smile, trying to joke, "I apparently have anxiety and paranoia to spare."

"Which would explain the spying," I noted. He moaned, "Look, I know I should be getting through remedial, but I just…"

He looked surprised when I didn't stop him, and finished, "I just can't help thinking something bad will happen, and I won't be around to protect you. I'm sorry, I just can't control the urge to check."

I punched him in the arm to take the sulk off his face and laughed, "What? C'mon how long am I able to stay mad at you?"

"Longest time on record is just over two weeks," he recalled, "And it was over Thanksgiving, too. You wouldn't even pass the salt."

"Hey, you almost caused me to lose my dog!" I reminded, though I was still smiling. His grin started to turn genuine as he replied, "That was an accident and you know it."

"Yeah, I do," I agreed. He requested, "Hey, if you don't have too much summer homework, can you help me out tonight? Struggling with decimals."

A nervous sort of chuckle left me as I explained, "Mark's the math whiz, not me."

"Oh sure. 'Hey, Mark. While your imaginary eye daggers are stabbing me in the heart, can you help me with two-point-six times one-point-four?' He would just as soon stick his own sword in his foot."

"He doesn't hate you-" Trace gave me a look of skepticism and I tried, "-he's just- protective of family, that's all."

"No, I'm pretty sure he hates me," he concluded, stuffing his hands in his pockets. We traded stories about our day until we reached the workshop. The walk was just over half a mile, about fifteen minutes at most when we were walking casually.

Garrett was showing his dragon Mescheaf affection, while Will and Divios were landing just behind them. They were the dragonriders of my mom's generation, and she was part of their team. My cousins and I were the team of our generation, and our dragons were probably already waiting inside the shop. Garrett and Will, being the remaining riders of their time, were our mentors when it came to elemental powers.

I didn't realize my dad was here at the workshop until he came striding up to us. He pulled Trace and Jamie aside to tell them, "Hey, your father called. Said your mother had a stroke-"

"A stroke?" Horror and confusion lit up Trace's eyes. He knew he didn't like the word, but it was clear he wasn't sure why. My dad continued, "He said it wasn't bad, but he took her to the hospital to be safe. He wanted me to bring you over when you got here."

"Can I come, too?" I asked. Dad denied, "Jamaica, you need to practice-"

"I've gotten better," I pleaded, "One day won't kill me! Please?"

He pursed his lips. Trace stepped up and defended, "The moral support would be nice, Sir."

My dad submitted, somewhat reluctantly, so Trace, Jamie, and I went racing toward my house, my Dad running after us. In minutes, we all scrambled into the car, me calling dibs for front seat. Trace rapped his knuckles against his thigh and bounced his leg, impatiently waiting as my dad rushed across the grass to get to the vehicle. Dad didn't say a word as he swung into the driver's seat, started the engine, and left the driveway. I twisted in my seat, and Trace's darting eyes locked on me a moment, his body stilling in self-consciousness for a few seconds. Then he was back to his nervous movements. Jamie was eerily calm, staring out the window like she was on a boring road trip. And no one talked.

When we arrived, Trace and Jamie were out of the car before I could even get my seatbelt off. My dad mumbled, "Christ-"

"I'll go after them," I assured, propelling myself out the door. By the time I caught up to the two, they had skidded to a stop at the reception desk. The lady at the desk had a thick, nasally New York accent as she put her hands up, saying, "Slow down, slow down! Who're you here to see?"

"Cecelia Maruken," Trace blurted, palms flattening on the counter. I came up behind him, holding his shoulder. I felt some of the tenseness leave him, and he slipped his hands back to his sides. The receptionist asked, "How do you know her?"

"These are her son and daughter," I explained as Dad finally walked up behind us. When the lady gave a look of doubt, Dad offered, "I have permission from Mr. Maruken to escort them. I can call and have him come down to confirm."

"There's no time," I heard Jamie whisper. She had her arms crossed, glancing around subtly at the other visitors in the waiting room. Dad already had the call ringing, and in the next five minutes, Jack Maruken himself came out to confirm our story, ushering us kids back to Mrs. Maruken's hospital room.

She reached out as her children ran to hug her. Jamie breathed, "We were worried."

"Are you okay?" Trace questioned, some panic still evident. His mother placed a hand on his cheek to calm him, and then began explaining what happened through sign language. I spotted Mr. Maruken leaving the room, and curiosity got the best of me. I snuck close to the door just as a doctor started talking, "- mini stroke causes little damage, usually, but can be a sign of something larger coming. I would like to discuss some options with you and your wife in private."

"Of course, of course," Mr. Maruken's voice swiftly consented. I got out of the way as they walked back in, though they probably knew I'd been eavesdropping. Mr. Maruken suggested, "Kids, why don't you go out in the hallway for a few minutes?"

"We just got here," Jamie protested. Mr. Maruken firmly stated, "This isn't up for discussion-"

"But Dad-"

"Trace," Their father gritted his teeth, and both shied away, exiting the room and taking me with them. The door closed behind us. Jamie folded her arms, mumbling, "This isn't right."

"They probably just need to talk about adult stuff," I tried, but she shook her head. "Not that. The stroke thing."

"What do you mean?"

"It just looks wrong," she thought, "Bruno disappeared last night, and the next day Mom's in the hospital. Something's going on-"

The hallway suddenly started to buzz, and workers in scrubs shoved past us into the room. Mr. Maruken wormed his way out and pulled the three of us further down the hall to get out of the way. Trace breathed, "Dad, what's going on, what's happening-?"

"It's another stroke, it will be handled-" A strange, terrifying screech came from the room, leading to faces of horror from all of us. Trace moved first, heading back to the room before his dad could stop him. I was right on his tail, but halted as the doctor nearly knocked me over. He cleared his throat and avoided eye contact as he slipped past me over to Mr. Maruken. More hesitant, I opened the door, giving space for the nurses to leave.

I swallowed when I turned into the room. Trace was alone, fists tightly curled around the sidebar of the bed.

"Trace," I whispered.

She...She's gone...

I put a hand on his shoulder, and he cringed. He was struggling to hold back the tears.

Trace, I'm so sorry.

I-I can't stay here. I can't-

He left the room before I could blink. I looked at Mrs. Maruken, Cecelia, and had to take a deep breath. There was no doubt that she was gone.

Mr. Maruken and Jamie rushed into the room, and I guess they knew the moment I glanced at them. Jamie broke into sobbing, her father taking her into his arms and trying to be strong. Nonetheless, his voice cracked as he requested that I go find his son. I nodded and hurried back out to the hallway.

Trace, where are you?

Leave me alone, Jamaica.

I leaned against the wall to get out of the way of a nurse.

Please, your dad told me to come find you-

My cell phone rang, and I fished it from my pocket. "Dad?"

"Hey, sweetie," he replied, *"Trace just walked back out into the waiting room. I haven't talked to him yet, is everything okay?"*

"No," I mumbled, "Call Mr. Maruken so he knows where to find us. I'll talk to Trace."

When I hung up, I raced back toward the entrance of the building. Just as I reached the doors out into the lobby, I slowed down and opened them quietly. The receptionist that had let us in looked up. Though she was in the middle of a call, she pointed over to Trace, sitting motionless in one of the plastic chairs. I cautiously approached and eased into the seat next to him. He croaked, "It's all my fault."

Tears streaked down his cheeks as he sniffled and fought even harder not to let it get the best of him. But it didn't work this time. He was crying now, whether he wanted to or not. I awkwardly circled my arms around him, and luckily, he responded by turning to me and pressing his forehead to my shoulder. The butterflies in my stomach burst to life again when his arms wrapped around my back. The little insects had never quite disappeared.

I squeezed his shoulders tighter as he fell apart, and I tried not to do so with him. The sounds of despair were enough to drag any sympathy I might have had in reserve out onto my face. I closed my eyes and, keeping my voice as even as I could, soothed, "It's going to be okay."

One Less Trainee

2

We eventually left the hospital, however much time later. Mr. Maruken decided to take his kids out of practice for the day, and drove home with them. I had to beg Dad to let me go back after I told him what happened. As I trudged down the hill, the clack of wooden weapons reached me.

Something whirred by my ear and popped against a tree. It was a stick with feathers on one end and a spongy cylinder on the other.

"Oh my gosh, Jamaica, I'm sorry!" Kaia called as she and Scarlet ran up to me. These two and Anna were a few friends I had enlisted to help the riders when needed. They certainly made practice interesting, if a little harder to navigate without getting a practice arrow to the head.

Kaia picked up her fake arrow, saying, "I was trying to hit Scar, but clearly, I missed. What's wrong?"

"N-Nothing," I muttered, mind only half there, "Go back to practice, and keep on it until five thirty, like usual."

"Where are you going?" Scarlet asked as I began walking again. They fell into step with me while I answered, "Workshop."

We had just reached the practice grounds when Scarlet asked, "Hey, Joey mentioned something about Trace and Jamie's mom being in the hospital. Is she okay?"

My lungs didn't want to cooperate as I informed, "No."

I got into the workshop before they could ask any more about it. "Jamaica?"

Anna stood in front of me, a wooden knife replica in her right hand. "There you are. I got back from my appointment early, but K.C. said you weren't here. Something about going to the hospital with your Dad-"

I put my hand over my face and tried to turn away, but she wouldn't let me. Holding my arm gently, she pressed, "What happened?"

My head bobbled a little helplessly before finally giving in, "Mr. Maruken took his wife to the hospital because she had a minor stroke, and-and-"

I was at a loss for words, "-I don't even know. We just heard a weird scream, Trace ran into the room, and by the time I got in...she died, Anna. One second she was there, she was fine, and the next..."

She comforted me, reading my emotions pretty easily. The fact was hitting me over and over again. Seeing Mrs. Maruken like that had left me a little dumbstruck.

"Anna," Joey ordered, sauntering up, "Get back to practice. I can take it from here."

Anna didn't move at first, but eventually opened the door and went to find a sparring partner. Joey took me by the shoulders and led me into the Sleeping Quarters, demanding, "I don't know what's going on, but it's draining you. Take a rest."

15

"But I need to practice," I protested as I plunked down on a cot. He insisted, "Not right now, you don't. Your head is too clouded. Stay here."

And with that, he strode back out into the main room. I laid down on the cot and proved him right as I fell asleep almost instantly. That didn't last long, though.

----0----

Kaia and Jamie crouched beside me. Trace was a short distance from us, tied to a tree. His clothes were bloody and ripped, and he was barely conscious. A man, an agent, approached, took a knife from his thigh-

"JAMAICA!!" I sat up as someone roared my name, and I knocked heads with Trace. A split-second view of ocean blue eyes, and I had my arms around his stomach, practically forcing the air from his lungs. He pried me off and grabbed my shoulders, murmuring, "You were screaming my name. Why were you screaming my name?"

"I-I was?" We stared at each other a moment, and then it was his turn to hug me. I inhaled sharply, realizing, "Your dad took you home. How are you here?"

His muscles tensed, and I heard the sob choked back into his throat as he laughed, "I'm good at sneaking off."

I steadily slipped back from the embrace, concern consuming me. He looked away, explaining quietly, "I had to get away. I just- I can't think about it right now. I can't think about..."

He gulped, so I finished, "Her."

Trying to even out his breath, he asserted, "Training takes up my focus. I need it right now."

I chewed the inside of my cheek, then agreed, "Me, too. Let's do it."

A smile popped on his mouth a little. We left the sleeping quarters and raced for the front door- and accidentally tackled Kaia on her way in. I groaned, "Sorry. You okay, Kaia?"

She puffed a dark curly lock out of her face and back into her giant splay of hair. "Peachy."

My friend shoved her way out from under Trace and me, continuing, "Don't tell us to get back to practice, it's five thirty."

Trace winced, so I quickly brushed off, "Fine, fine. Go ahead inside."

"Actually," Scarlet spoke, "Anna's grandma is running late again, and my dad got held up. So, we were thinking of taking a walk through the woods."

My head dropped before I permitted, "Go ahead. But take your real weapons with you."

They rushed inside, one to grab a knife, the other a sword. I looked over at Trace's grimace, and suggested, "Why don't you and I go one-on-one? It hasn't been just us in a while."

He slowly bobbed his head and scrambled up. I was quick to follow. He was smiling, even if half-heartedly, and I couldn't ask for more.

An Unbrotherly Reunion

3

It had been about a day, Bruno knew that much. Most of the time, he pretended to be unconscious around the agents that had captured him, hoping to gather information, but that had proved fruitless. The men that captured him- one wasn't really a man at all. He was just a boy, likely about the kids' age, and fairly scrawny. His elder had no above average physique either, and was little more than a pilot of the helicopter transporting their captive. Bruno, easily stronger than both of them, could escape with no trouble. But if he had been taken, with little reinforcements to guard his movements…that meant James wanted to see him personally, for whatever reason.

A different presence drifted through Bruno's mind, so he steeled himself.

What do you want, James?
Now is that any way to greet your older brother?
My question stands.

Bruno ignored what clearly felt like his brother relishing the moment, waiting impatiently for him to get on with it.

Surely, you're aware that you act only as bait.

Naturally. It's one of the only things I could imagine, coming from the mind of a psychopath such as yourself.

Watch what you say, little brother. You wouldn't want to risk young Joseph paying for your words, now would you?

Bruno paused, fear pitting in his stomach.

What did you do to him, James?

Not what I did. One of the agents bringing you to me has allowed me control over the youngest of your partners. A certain device around the wrist that can emit low frequencies of electricity through the wearer. Just enough to make them endure pain.

Hasn't he been through enough without your torture?

Please, dear brother, you know my answer to that.

Pain licked up Bruno's arm, surely meant as insight to what Joey could be feeling at the moment. He bit back the familiar discomfort.

James. I will not fight against you. But Joey holds no place in our feud. I only ask for mercy on him.

The sparking tingle left, but his arm twitched for several seconds after.

Never did I think I would see the day that you would grovel once more.

I am not groveling. Pleading, maybe.

I presume you will treat me with respect, then, if you will only go so far.

Only to assure Joey's safety.

Very well. Be sure to say hello. You have family closer than you might imagine.

The presence left. Bruno had long dreaded the nightmares of his past, most inflicted by his brother. But he was to be damned if James spread such trauma to someone else. The riders couldn't be stopped from confronting his brother, but Joey was unconnected to the deep family rift between them. And Bruno would ensure that didn't change.

Only then did the last comment hit him. What had James meant by family being close?

"Hey, it's time to get moving," the boy of the two agents hissed, patting Bruno's cheeks. It was hardly a slap, but the boy wasn't gentle in the slightest. Bruno pretended to wake up for takeoff, James' mention quickly falling to the back of his mind.

Sparks

4

"Time to go in, yet?" I laughed. Trace and I were both sweaty and panting, having gone back and forth nonstop for- heck, I'd lost track of the time. Garrett and Will hadn't been very happy with me skipping bending practice, but they didn't protest.

"I could do this all day," Trace smiled through his breathing. It had done him some good to get away from reality for a little while. But the sky was starting to dim, and with Bruno missing, Joey would want us in soon. Trying to get him in willingly, I offered, "If you go in, I'll give you a kiss."

The smile wavered slightly. He knew exactly what I was doing. He sighed, "You drive a hard bargain, Zwivelle. Although…"

He suddenly shot forward and pecked me on the lips, "If I steal that kiss, then I s'pose our deal is off, isn't it?"

He giggled as I shook my head, submitting, "Fine, but if we get called inside, we have to go."

"Deal." He swung the wooden sword, and I immediately ducked. The sword came back, and I caught it with my fake dagger. Here, we reached a stalemate, equally matched in strength. He warned, "I'm gonna win!"

"In your dreams!" I dared. He challenged, "You can't push my weapon away, what are you gonna-?"

I initially thought to threaten spitting in his eye, but then I had a better idea as payback. I pulled his head down and kissed him nice and long, trying not to laugh. The pressure against my blade relaxed, meaning I'd gotten his guard down. I released him, and pounced. We were on the ground in seconds, me sitting on top of him. He had let go of his weapon in his surprise, and I had mine hovering over his throat by the time he stretched an arm out for it. I snickered, "Gotcha."

"You tricked me," he snorted, and I claimed, "I was stealing my kiss back!"

As we continued the playful argument, we started laughing, to the point that we couldn't form sentences. I fell over and lay next to him, trying to breathe. Trace calmed faster than me, looking up at the sky. Tonight's sunset wasn't much, maybe a little bit of yellow and gold. But Trace stared at it with the corners of his mouth up, completely peaceful.

A scream came from inside the workshop, and after a split second for shock, Trace and I got to our feet and rushed back inside to a bad scene. Joey had collapsed, and was now writhing on the floor, holding one of his forearms. The device's screen had gone blue. "Joey!"

I slid next to him on my knees as Trace demanded, "Get it off him-!"

"I'll try-"

"Jamaica, stop!" Mark said when he burst through the door and saw me. Trace open his mouth to yell, but Mark harshly spat,

"It's electrocuting him! If she touches it while it's on, it might do the same to her!"

Trace fought himself a second, but retreated in a smaller voice, "He's right. You'll have to wait until it turns off."

Luckily, it only took another second before the whirring sound shut off, along with the blue light. K.C. just about barreled through Mark, Will and Garrett nearly squashing her. Joey was dazed, and I kept him lying down when I saw that his arm was still spastic. Mark knelt next to me, picking up Joey's wrist. My cousin's jaw tightened. "Good thing you didn't touch it. He's probably been seriously burned, it's so hot."

"Well, we can't do anything to help unless Jamaica can get it off," Andrew stated. The remaining three blacksmiths kept their distance, in hopes that we would be able to do something. Michael suggested, "Mark, you're able to absorb the fire from the forge at night. Do you think you could take the heat away?"

Mark's head rocked a little, tongue flashing out to the side of his lips and back in a half second. "Maybe."

He wrapped his hands around the device, staring at it intensely. His hands smoked just a little, but he let go a moment later, saying, "It should be cool enough now."

I tapped the tip of my finger against it, only to find it was ice cold. Setting to work, I concentrated on the molecules of the strap, moving them around until the polarity changed and the sides popped apart. The device didn't budge, and my cousin quickly noted the skin underneath, sure that it was at least a second-degree burn. Trying to ignore the fact, I carefully rested my hand over the top, focusing on reforming the end of the needle in Joey's skin. The smith gasped, and Mark caught the good arm from shoving my hand away.

"Mark," He looked at me, prepared. I murmured, "if it's stuck to his skin, I can't get it off."

"K.C.," he tossed over his shoulder. She got down on my other side, and I explained the situation. She formed a free-floating orb of water and slipped Joey's hand through, explaining, "Now, I'm not sure that this will work, but I remember that you're supposed to soak burns in room temperature water. So, I figure maybe if I do that, it'll loosen the device away from his wrist."

I could see Joey starting to gather his bearings, breathing shallowly as his dark eyes darted between the three of us. K.C. ordered Mark and me, "Hold his wrists. Joey, try not to move, this will probably hurt."

The man's eyes widened just before K.C.'s fingers started moving in such a motion that, watching how the device started to come off, looked like she was shaving it away from his skin. Joey's arms contracted, and he closed his eyes. K.C.'s hands came together, and she steadily pushed, the device sliding away from the smith's arm entirely.

I shivered at the ring of red, blistered skin underneath. Trace hadn't had that, and it made me wonder how the composition of the device had changed since then.

The water vanished, the device falling to the floor as Andrew hauled his youngest partner up. Joey slurred that he was fine, but was soon handed off to Jeff, who brought him into the Infirmary and closed the door. There was a long pause before K.C. exhaled, "Well, if we weren't sure who took Bruno before, we are now."

"The Emperor's back," Mark growled, but no sooner did the last word leave him, the door burst in once again, Anna and Scarlet smacking into Garrett's spine. They slammed the door into its frame, Anna panicking, "They're coming, they're-"

"Who's coming?" Will asked, to which she replied, "Agents, they're-they're-"

"We saw them while we were walking," Scarlet tried to get the information across, "They looked like they were preparing. Of course, when we saw them, they saw us, so-"

A loud thump hit the door. But it was much heavier than a weapon, or even a fist. It sounded like a body. When the thunderous dragon roar blasted into our ears, it became pretty clear what happened. Andrew commanded, "Grab your weapons. The dragons may be protecting us, but the perimeter still needs to be secured."

Everyone went into a flurry of limbs as we followed orders, and soon, we were slowly creeping out of the workshop. Aside from the mangled body slumped against the frame, the clearing was quiet.

Jamaica, get back inside!

Mugireti, it's okay. Safety in numbers, right?

Mugireti, my dragon, looked at me skeptically. His eyes were just as blue as mine, his scales the same color of my brown hair. Except for the darker belly, eye mask and wing membranes, of course. His gaze returned to watching the forest for movement.

There were six. We managed to get two, but they're really good at hiding-

My breath caught in my throat as someone snatched my arm and pulled me back. A cold edge touched my neck. The others were quick to notice, and Mark bared his teeth, hands sparking as he threatened, "Think really hard about what you're doing. You take so much as one step-"

"What will you do?" The sneer came behind me, "If you attack me, you could hurt her-"

His shoulder flinched, and there was a flare of heat near my ear. My cousin retorted, "You wanna bet on it?"

For a second or two, all I could hear was the steady breathing of my captor under the shakiness of my own. Trace

25

finally stepped forward, cautious when the grip on my arm tightened. He offered, "Take me."

"Like hell-"

"Listen to me!" Trace commanded, a sudden authority washing over him, "If you try to leave with her, you won't make it out of here alive. If you take me, you can walk, for now. And keeping me captive will cause the rest of my team to follow. You still get your target."

I could see his eyes searching, wanting it to work. His body was rigid, the wait for an answer killing him.

I was shoved sideways, my head making contact with a tree trunk. Through blurred vision I saw the captor hold Trace back from the rest of the group rushing toward me. Though I found it more disturbing now than surprising, I heard my mother's voice scream my name. How many times would I hear that?

----0----

I woke with a start, half expecting to find my wrists handcuffed and metal bars around me. But to my relief, I recognized the inside of the workshop instantly. The side of my head blossomed with pain, and I was quick to place a hand over the spot.

"Hey, you're up," someone whispered. K.C. knelt next to me, adding, "How does your head feel?"

Dizzy and a little nauseous. "Fine. Nasty bruise, I bet."

"It could be worse." As I start to remember why my head hurt, I remembered something else. "Trace-"

"The agents have him," she sighed, combing red hair away from her face. Most of the blue hair dye mistake from last year had grown out, so now she had areas of dark green tips. Not one her most attractive looks, but she made it work all the same. I mumbled, "Right. How did they find us, anyway?"

26

"That's what everyone is still trying to figure out. Andrew, Michael, and Jeff have been looking for any new trackers, but there's nothing yet."

"Are the agents still nearby?" She shook her head. "Garrett went to check it out with Anna, but they only found a pile of burned wood from a campfire."

I bit the inside of my lip. "Then I guess we're playing follow the leader."

"Jamaica, you almost got killed last time-"

"I know. But how else are we supposed to save Trace and Bruno?" She pouted a little, but nodded. "It's past ten. Mark and I probably need to go home, now that you're okay."

"Mark's still here?"

"Yeah," she answered, worried, "We had to force him to stay in another room. He was freaking out too much for Jeff to focus on examining your head."

K.C. stood up and went to the sleeping quarters, swinging the door in and making a grand gesture with her arm. In seconds, Mark hurried out, spotted me, and suffocated me in a hug, saying, "Thank god."

"Mark, you're strangling me," I choked, causing him to shift back very fast. "Sorry. They wouldn't let me-"

"I heard."

"Mark, c'mon, we have to go home so our parents can kill us for being out late." He pursed his lips in annoyance, but asked me, "Can you make it home alright?"

I assured, "Mugireti will be more than willing to escort me."

He inhaled and looked away, rising and following K.C. outside. I heard two dragons take off as the larger outside door opened, and a familiar head curved in. Mugireti.

Are you alright, Jamaica?

I've been worse.

And then came the familiar chiding look.

That does not matter, nor does it answer my question.

I'm okay, aside from the giant bruised lump on the side of my head.

Your father wanted me to bring you home when you were able to go. Is it that time, yet?

I should be just fine getting up.

Well, I tried standing up. And I would've been fine if Joey hadn't startled me by commanding, "Sit back down."

I landed on my butt none too gracefully, and glared as he crouched down next to me. He explained, "You're not going anywhere until I can make sure your brain hasn't sustained serious damage."

"So, a concussion," I snipped. He calmly said, "Yes."

"Why can't you have Jeff do it? You're supposed to be resting."

"Because Jeff may be good at medical knowledge," he pulled a pocket flashlight out, "but I'm the one that taught him. Besides, I made the others go to bed to get rest themselves."

I felt like I was at a doctor checkup as he performed a bunch of tests to make sure my reaction times were normal. "I heard about Trace…I'm sorry."

"I'm leaving in the morning," I blurted. The thought had crossed my mind, and apparently, I couldn't stop it from jumping out of my mouth. Joey froze a moment, but decided, "No, you're not."

"Joey-"

"Not without help," he clarified, "Mugireti, inform the team. Meet back here at nine o'clock tomorrow morning."

My dragon nodded. And in his concentration, his floppy ears unfurled into satellite-dish-like shapes. Joey turned back to me, saying, "You can stand up now. He'll probably be ready to take you home in a minute. I'm going to get some sleep, and I recommend you do, too. Good night."

"Good night." He walked back to the sleeping quarters while I hauled myself to my feet and shuffled over to Mugireti. His ears returned to normal after a little while, and I climbed on his back so he could walk home.

Are you tired?

Not really. Those few hours of unconsciousness gave me a nice nap.

Mugireti's lungs expanded in a sigh, and I felt like I might vibrate right off him.

Try to get some sleep, then. You now have a very important meeting tomorrow.

We were quiet as he plodded through the forest, curving around to the back of the house and to my window. I slid down to the ground, then gave my dragon an innocent smile.

Help me up to my bedroom?

I'm going to get in trouble with your father again.

Please?

He rolled his eyes, but nonetheless lowered his head to the ground for me to clamber on top. The trick was to maintain balance as he lifted his head, that way I could slide my window back to crawl into my room on the second floor. I reached out, giving a few pushes and pulls that tried to take my balance, and managed to open my window. Cautiously stretching between Mugireti's forehead and the sill, I tumbled into my room, with squeaking protests from my mattress. I stuck a thumbs up out, then closed the pane as Mugireti lay down to sleep.

"Hey! Down, girl! Down, down, Dragon, no!" I squealed, my Great Dane, Dragon, having jumped on my bed, now attempting to lick me to death. Dad was pulling her off a second later, scolding, "Jamaica, I told you not to climb through your window! You know it's dangerous."

29

"Sorry, Dad," I replied, trying to be as genuine as possible, "I just wanted to go straight to bed."

"Joey came up the hill and told me everything. Bruno, Mrs. Maruken, Trace," he ground his teeth a little, "I know the whole story. How's your head?"

"Sore," I shrugged. As my mind played back through it all, my mood sank astonishingly lower than it was. Seeing this, my dad sat down on the bed next to me and wrapped an arm around my shoulders. With a small squeeze, he coaxed, "It'll all work out. I promise."

We said our good nights, and he dragged Dragon out of the room, closing the door behind himself and her. I sluggishly changed into my pajamas, setting my dagger and belt on my night table. Finally, I pulled my comforter and sheets back to collapse in bed and get some relief from this stressful day.

The Cavalry

5

Are you ready yet?
Almost.

I had just pulled my socks on when Dad opened the door to my room, Dragon wriggling past him to give me morning slobber. Dad pulled her back, saying, "You're up early for the first day of summer."

His voice was somber and quiet, telling me he was completely aware of what I was doing and where I was going. I tried, "Dad- I-"

"I know," he cut me off, guarding his voice, "And I hate that I can't stop you."

I got up and hugged him, feeling a hand press against my upper back. Starting to crack, he asked, "You're absolutely sure?"

I thought about it, wanting to give him an answer that was true, and finally pulled away, declaring, "I wouldn't go back there if I didn't think it was worth it."

He swallowed hard. "Then put all of that training to good use."

"I-I will." I grabbed my shoes, belt, and dagger, and shimmied past him, avoiding eye contact. I clopped downstairs and opened the front door to find Mugireti waiting.

Why don't you have your shoes on?

"Don't worry about it." I sat down on the porch steps, stuffing my feet into my shoes.

Did you brush your teeth?

"Yes."

Hair?

"Yeah."

Deodorant?

"None of this will matter in a few days, mind you." One scaly brow rose. "Yes, I used deodorant. Why are you suddenly worried about it?"

I just figure you should be hygienically sound as often as possible.

I rolled my eyes, grumbling, "We have more important things to worry about."

We walked down the hill my family's house sat on, and through the surrounding forest. Before I knew it, we were approaching the workshop. The other dragons were waiting outside, likely on surveillance after yesterday. K.C. wasn't here yet, seeing as no orange dragon named Pirsniketi was here either. My mother's dragon Pashince wasn't present, which didn't surprise me. After Mom's disappearance, he had kept to himself so much that he was rarely seen. And even with most of his cluster back, that hadn't changed.

Mugireti joined his kin to keep watch while I went inside. Of our little band, K.C. and Scarlet were both missing- but there was one extra body. "Mr. Maruken?"

Mr. Maruken stood with his daughter near a wall, both quiet. He granted, "Good morning, Jamaica."

"What-What are you doing here?" It wasn't abnormal for Trace's parents to come to the workshop. Cecelia had helped with training, and Mr. Maruken felt it was a good idea to learn some form of self-defense. But Cecelia was gone. And this wasn't training.

His eyes were tired and somewhat dead as he encouraged Jamie to go talk to Garrett. Trace had a lot of physical traits from his dad, so it was weird to think that Trace could look like that someday. Mr. Maruken turned back to me and whispered, "Jamaica, I just lost my wife yesterday, and for the sake of my kids, I have to be strong. It's a difficult fact to come to terms with, but not-"

He paused to build his composure back up, "-not unexpected. The Emperor knows us by name and face. It shouldn't have been a surprise that he would eventually come back."

"So, he did do it, then?" I murmured. He explained, "The doctor said she showed signs of another stroke, but died swiftly, and- in extreme pain…"

He quieted, but hadn't answered me. Not really. "You should be home taking time to mourn-"

"I lost my wife. I'm not losing my son, too," he finalized. I glanced at my shoes and walked away. K.C. and Scarlet both arrived in the next couple of minutes, and I started counting heads. Ten, so two to each dragon. Everyone quickly split up and began mounting. Joey caught my arm just as Jamie and I started to climb Mugireti's foreleg. "Jamaica."

I stopped, and his eyes darted away, like he was trying to think of what to say. He finally looked at me again, warning, "Be careful. We want Bruno to come back safely- we want you to do the same. Understand?"

I nodded, and he let go, allowing me to get settled into the niche behind Mugireti's neck, Jamie sliding down from her perch on the dragon's back to be right behind me. We waited until everyone was secure and ready to go, then took off into the morning.

----0----

I think it's time to land. The sun's been down for a while. It's up to you.

Mugireti was right. It was so dark, I couldn't even see the forest until I felt a tree scrape my leg. As the others landed, Mugireti sent a thought to everyone.

Don't start a fire yet. I'm sensing footsteps not far away.

He started to leave the group, and I went with him.

Where are you going?

Scouting.

Mugireti, you're a dragon. Whoever it is will see you for sure.

He stopped.

Then get a scout team together.

"What are you doing?" Jamie asked behind me. I spun around and asked, "You wanna do some scouting?"

"Uh, sure." I called Kaia over, too, telling the others we wouldn't be long. We crept wordlessly, and Mugireti stopped a few hundred yards away from the movement he sensed. I started to feel it as we got closer, seeing fire light. The three of us dropped to the bushes when we were close enough to see. There were four men around the fire, and near the shadows- Trace. He was tied to a tree, several bloody rips in his shirt. One of the agents got up, and I caught sight of the knife attached to his thigh. Knowing Jamie would react, I crawled toward her. Just as the knife came out of its

34

sheath, I grabbed her and put a hand over her mouth. She struggled to get free as her brother cried out.

"Jamie, stop!" I hissed, "If they see us, they'll capture us, too! We can't help him if they have us!"

She curled her legs in and kicked me in the stomach, scrambling away.

Trace, are you there?

Jamaica?

His voice was weak, even telepathically.

Jamie's headed toward you. Kaia and I are right behind her, but make sure she stays hidden.

What are you doing here? They'll kill you if you get caught.

We're not leaving without you.

"We have to get out of here-"

"Kaia, Trace is right there, with no way to defend himself, we can't just leave him. Now c'mon, we have to go after Jamie."

We snuck after her and quickly found the twelve-year-old madly working at the knots around her brother's wrists. "Jamie-"

"How do you untie these things?!" she groaned under her breath. Kaia suggested, "I used to be in girl scouts. Maybe I can help."

She got to work, and I silently slipped forward, whispering, "Hey."

Trace looked over, and the corner of his mouth inched up. His lip was split, and the smile only pulled it open more. But I was more concerned with the blood on his body. He noticed, and croaked softly, "They're not as bad as they look."

"We'll talk about it later," I managed to push out, "The goal is just to get you to safety-"

"Hey you!" One of the agents yelled. I muttered, "Crap."

"Run!" Trace ordered, but I looked back, saying, "Kaia-"

"Just a few more seconds-"

"We don't have a few more seconds-!"

35

"We're not leaving my brother-!" I panicked and threw an air barrier up, wind whirring around us in a small cylinder. I watched the agents try to get through for a moment before Kaia piped, "I got it!"

"Good, now how do we get out of here?" Jamie snapped, keeping her eyes on the agents that now surrounded the barrier. The four were pacing like animals, waiting for us. I thought, "Mugireti, maybe?"

"We can't give them a reason to go after the others," Trace advised, achingly rubbing his wrists, "If they think they can capture the dragons, they'll do exactly that."

A hand got through the barrier momentarily, and I gulped. Jamie inquired, "Trace, can you run?"

He whined a little before, "It's debatable."

"Maybe if we run different directions-" I got woozy a moment, and the barrier weakened. I told the others, "I can't hold this much longer."

There was a pause before Trace muttered, "Put it down."

"Trace-"

"I have an idea. Put it down, let them get us, and I'll try to take it from there." I was reluctant, but did as he said. The tallest of the agents snatched my arm and twisted it behind me, a knife guarding my neck. He demanded, "Now which one is the rider?"

The man restraining Trace jutted a salt and pepper beard at me, sneering, "Her."

He only said one word, but I recognized his voice as that of the captor at the workshop. Kaia shouted, "You're horrible people!"

"You're helping fugitives," my agent retorted, but Trace was quick to grab attention, "So that gives you the right to kill Jamaica? Because she's a rider?"

"Shut up," his captor grumbled, knuckles connecting with my boyfriend's stomach. Kaia's agent growled, "Dan, enough."

36

"She's fourteen," Trace pushed out, "How do you plan to tell your families you killed a fourteen-year-old girl just to see them?"

The men behind Kaia and Jamie shifted uneasily. Trace dealt, "You keep me, you take Jamaica, and you let these two go to pass on the message."

"What message?" my guard spat. I saw a smile suppressed on Trace's face. "You have the main target. Our team will be careful, and you can lead all of them to the Emperor."

I could just picture the contemplation, and my agent finally huffed, "Let 'em go. And you two- scram."

"I'm not leaving my brother!" Jamie argued. Trace maintained, "Go, Stickers. I'll be fine."

She glowered at him, but his expression made her comply.

"Jamie, come on," Kaia urged. Jamie trudged after her silently. My agent let me go, but I shot away when he reached for my dagger. "The dagger stays with me."

"You're not in a position to make demands-"

"The only way you're getting this dagger is off my dead body!" I declared, though I flinched when he readied the knife that had been at my throat. He threatened through his teeth, "That can be arranged."

"If you kill her, the Emperor kills you," Trace quickly reasoned, "It's common sense. She's his target, not yours. You kill her, and he'll go after everyone you love before ending you."

The tenseness in the man's shoulders didn't ease, and finally, the youngest of the four agents touched his shoulder, saying, "It's not worth it, Cory."

After another second, Cory pulled his shoulder away, glaring at his partner. "It better not be. We leave in the morning."

He stormed back to the fire, the young agent and the third following. I noticed that the third one had darker skin then the others, more like Mark's. "Ya know, if it were up to me-"

37

Trace got shoved into me, just about making me topple as his captor smirked, "-you'd already be dead. Count yourself lucky, little miss."

My boyfriend had his arm across me, watching the man closely as he sauntered back to the fire. And that arm was what I caught when he stumbled forward. "Are you okay?"

"Just a little light-headed," he brushed off. I took one look at his shirt and said, "You've probably lost enough blood to cause that. Sit down, I think I remember how Mugireti makes his wrap."

"Okay, so the one that wants us dead is Dan?" I asked, Trace nodded as I tried to remember, "And then the really tall one is Cory. He was the one with the knife."

"Yep," Trace confirmed, a little bit of defense in his voice. I continued, "Fernando is the one with brown skin, and Ed is the young one who talked Cory down?"

"Right. He seems to have the most caution of them all. Cory hates riders for one reason or another, I haven't heard him say-"

"And Dan just wants blood for no apparent reason at all," I grumbled. Trace nodded, crossing his arms. He gasped, and I batted them away. While I had been able to wrap up the bad areas (mostly long, shallow surface cuts on his chest), I couldn't provide any pain killer.

I yawned, and he murmured, "You're tired. Get some rest."

"I'm okay, really-"

"Jamaica," I stopped at the softness of the tone, "Chances are, they won't hurt you. I've made sure of it. And hopefully, I've made sure they won't go after however many dragons you brought."

"Five," I sighed. He stated just above a whisper, "You're sleep-deprived. Go to sleep."

Feeling the sleepiness start to set in, I twisted my belt around, so my dagger was between us, breathing, "Don't let them take it."

"Never," was the reply. I leaned my head gingerly on his shoulder, avoiding what wounds I could, and drifted off to sleep.

"Jamaica," someone breathed, shaking my shoulder. I blearily opened my eyes to see Trace and morning light. He hurried, "It's time to go."

He led me, still tired and confused, to a helicopter, and in another minute, we were airborne.

----0----

"Mark, take it easy!" K.C. pleaded, grabbing his fist before he could shoot another stream of fire through camp. He was livid at the thought that Jamaica was in danger, and hadn't slept at all because of it. How could Mugireti have been so careless-?

Mark.

Not now, Beuti-

Mark.

A black scaled head appeared in front of him, dark eyes visible in a white mask.

Your temper is raging. If you aren't careful, you're going to hurt someone.

I'd like to hurt him- that stupid, blonde-

Trace has been nothing but trustworthy and helpful, Mark. I don't believe you are rightfully hateful towards him.

You've always said that. Now he's convinced her to be a captive with him.

Beuti sighed. K.C., having realized they were talking, had gone back over to Pirsniketi.

Mark, he is part of the team now.

He's not part of our cluster. He will never be part of that.

Beuti brought her nose up to his hand, and he felt calmer. It was a natural effect for him, anger washing away at the sense of their bond.

A cluster has limits. A team does not. And right now, this team needs a leader.

We have Garrett.

Mescheaf has told me many times that Garrett does not plan to step in unless he needs to. He wants our team to grow on our own.

Mark looked around, catching himself licking his lips. The group had collectively started to wake up, and someone would have to get them going soon. The helicopter had only taken off about twenty minutes ago, but if they let it get too far ahead, Jamaica would reach the OAD before everyone. And Mark didn't want to imagine what would happen in that situation.

As the others started to gather, Mark pushed into the middle and called, "Listen up! We're taking off in five minutes! If you have business to do, do it now!"

"We just woke up, Mark," Anna yawned. He walked up until they were face to face. Or rather nose to chin, seeing as he was a little taller. "I'm not letting whoever took Trace take Jamaica too. Are you with me, or not?"

An intimidating steel appeared in her eyes, and he failed to resist clenching his jaw. She hissed, "You wanna go? Then let's *go*."

She turned and stormed towards Beuti. Mark avoided the eyes of the other riders as the rest of the group reluctantly followed Anna's lead.

What did you do?

I got them moving.

Mark walked back over and began to climb up her leg when a sneaker nearly popped him in the nose. He glared at Anna who scowled right back. "Let me get on my dragon."

"If you think for one millisecond that I wouldn't do everything I can to save Jamaica, you're an idiot. She's my best friend-"

"And she's my cousin," he retorted, "Now move your foot, or I'm breaking it."

She stared a moment to see if he was serious, then hugged her foot back to Beuti's spine.

He swung his leg up into the niche behind his dragon's neck, ignoring the words that spilled out of Anna's mouth. He waited impatiently, and in the next few minutes, they were chasing the helicopter.

Four Agents

6

The sun was still high when we landed, though there was no explanation given as to what made us stop. Trace and I were more than compliant with exiting the copter, earning nasty looks from the agents. Trace shot the look right back, unfazed by them. I quickly scaled a tree nearby, Trace climbing right after me. And luckily for us, it took a small boost of air to get to the lowest branch. Cory hopped from our transportation yelling, "Get down here!"

"Brutes!" I braved, though it made me sure that I would pay for it. He growled back, "Watch your mouth!"

"We'll say whatever we want!" Trace dared, "The Emperor won't let you hurt her, and she won't let you hurt me!"

"Cory, just leave it be-"

"Since when did you take the fugitive's side, Ed-?!"

"I-I'm not, it's just-"

"Stay out of it!" Cory spat, lips curled back. I asked softly, "Why is he so aggressive?"

Trace shrugged, though his brow was knit as well. "I don't know, but it sure isn't normal- Jamaica-? Hey- get back up here!"

"I just- maybe I can talk to them."

"Doubt it," he scoffed, but he didn't make any move to stop me as I climbed down to the lowest branch. Cory bitterly puffed, "If you're coming down, then don't stop short."

"I'm good, thanks," I nervously replied. How Trace was so calm with his backtalk was beyond my understanding.

"Fine. If you won't come down on your own, I'll make you." I hadn't expected his jump to be enough to catch the branch, nor did I expect that the tips of his fingers would hold so well. He managed to heave himself up and was soon balancing about halfway down the branch, edging toward me. I pressed my back to the trunk, too petrified to remember that I'd just flown up the branches a moment ago. Bark cracked above us, and Trace was suddenly at my aid, blocking Cory. He panted, "Don't...you...*dare*."

Cory was able to grab him by the collar, and both lost their balance, hitting the ground pretty hard. Trace briefly got the upper hand, throwing a few good punches before Ed ripped him away. I thought for sure Trace would get hit, but Ed ordered, "Get in the tree! Now! Get up there!"

"Jamaica!" I impulsively gave Trace a boost, and he bounced a little, crouching on a branch just a little higher than mine. And just in time, the other two agents had come running from the pilot and copilot seats. Fernando cried, "What happened?!"

Ed wasn't listening. He grabbed Cory by the shirt and scolded, "That is exactly what you deserve for messing with a rider. Get yourself under control."

43

The youngest agent explained the situation, causing Dan to send a mean smile up to Trace. Trace mumbled, "C'mon, let's get higher- Jamaica?"

I was still staring at Ed. It didn't seem to fit that he had wanted Trace back in the tree before his partners arrived. He was an agent after all.

Jamaica, where are you?

Mugireti?

Who else? Don't answer that. Where are you?

We just landed.

Oh, good. I stopped feeling the vibrations and got worried.

"Jamaica," Trace tapped my shoulder. I touched my temple, saying, "Mugireti."

Are you close?

We've been flying about half an hour behind you. We'll be landing a few minutes short just to stay hidden.

So, you're leading the brigade now?

Surprisingly, no. Mark took charge.

I glanced at Trace, who waited expectantly.

If that's true, Trace may not be getting out of here any time soon.

I'm sure Beuti talked him down.

"Jamaica, come on. Before Cory gets his courage up again." I began climbing and trying to talk at the same time.

Maybe she talked to him, but I don't think that means he dislikes Trace any less.

Oh, give him a vote of confidence.

My vote of confidence goes towards assuming my cousin won't kill my boyfriend-

My leg kicked a tree branch and the pain crossed the connection to Mugireti.

What happened?

Trace and I are staying in a tree to keep our distance from the agents. My leg just hit a branch, I'm fine.

Well, if you stay in the tree, I can come through and make quick work of those apes. Little bit of mauling should do the trick-

Mugireti.

What?

I noticed Ed placing a hand on the tree, closing his eyes. It almost seemed like he was listening for something.

Hey, Mugireti, I gotta go. Hold off on the mauling until you get a full plan.

"What's he doing?" I inquired, watching the agent carefully. Trace deflected, "Does it matter?"

"It's just…weird, I guess. He doesn't act like the others."

"What do you mean?"

"He's relatively nice to us."

"He's an agent."

"Am I wrong?" Trace's shoulders fell a little as he looked at Ed with me, thinking aloud, "I s'pose he is less harsh. But that could just be because he's young."

"How old is he?"

"Early twenties at latest." I glanced up at my boyfriend and smirked, "Another talent you picked up on the run?"

He nonchalantly answered, "You can tell a lot about someone by their age alone. How much they're willing to help you, what you can take-"

His eyes grew, and he pursed his lips, "-and other things."

"Uh-huh," I mused. It didn't bother me as much as it probably should have that Trace used to beg and steal just to stay alive when he was a little kid. I just accepted it and moved on.

I flinched as Ed's fingertips suddenly raked down the bark and he shouted up, "Come down here."

"I'm not causing any trouble up here!" I replied, an anxious lump forming in my throat. He came right back with, "I know you're not, but come down anyway."

Trace held my arm, protesting, "Jamaica-"

"Trace, he may be an agent, but it seems like he wants to help us."

"We can't trust him!"

"We have to." I gazed at his features screwed tight in worry and disagreement. "Look, I know he's an agent, but my gut is telling me we should at least listen to what he has to say. Has my gut been wrong before?"

His expression turned incredibly cynical, so I edited, "Okay wrong question. But can we at least have some faith?"

His hand flexed a little before he committed, "Fine."

We made our way down the branches, stopping at the lowest ones. Trace pushed, "What do you want?"

"The both of you need to get out of here-"

"Why, so you can capture us again-?"

"Let me speak for two seconds, damn it!" He hissed at Trace, who immediately shut up. "Listen, Dan and I are just like you. We're both able to hear animals, alright? Dan went off the deep end a long time ago because of it, and I've been keeping it a secret."

"Why are you telling us?" Trace questioned. Ed replied, "Because your group just landed, and he went after them-"

"Hey," Cory strode up behind Ed, fuse still burning, "I thought you said you weren't siding with *them*."

Ed shoved him, reprimanding, "Dan is a predator going after those kids just because he thinks he can! You know that, Cory!"

"We are under orders!" Cory snarled back, but Ed roared, "*Orders*?! We're not killers, you bastard!"

46

As the two started to scream over one another, Trace batted at my shoulder and jabbed a thumb toward the woods. I nodded, and we quietly circled to the opposite side of the tree, carefully jumping down.

Mugireti, there's an agent headed for you, and he's out for blood.

Why?

I don't know!

Trace and I ducked and dodged through the trees, trying to find Dan before he found the others. Trace hollered, "Where is he?"

"How should I know?!" We kept running, and I just happened to catch a black and white wing flutter. "Trace, slow down, slow-"

The ground shook as a dragon landed nearby, tripping us both up. I landed on my hip, and Trace flat on his chest, letting out a small yelp. I roughly pushed myself up, saying, "We have to keep moving."

Biting back the obvious pain, Trace pushed himself to his feet, and we sprinted the last short way until we just about flattened ourselves into Beuti. Two voices adlibbed my name, and I found myself suddenly sandwiched between Mark and Anna. I wriggled out of the hold to explain what was going on, but it didn't end up mattering. Close by, two bodies fell from Mugireti's back, a short-lived struggle between them.

"Let me go!" Someone screamed. Trace inhaled sharply and ran towards them, Mark, Anna, and me right on his tail. We found Jamie on top of Dan, arms easily pinned to her sides as he kept her back pressed to his chest. Despite the knife at her neck, she was squirming like no tomorrow. Dan cackled, "You keep moving, this knife will do the work for me!"

"Let her go," Trace snarled scarily calm, venom in his voice. He lunged, wrestling Dan's arm loose enough for his sister

47

to slip free. He stumbled back again with a new cut just below his shoulder. Dan eyed me, and in a flash, I was ducking and dodging him, losing ground all over the place as I ran away from him. The others tried to help, but he was unfortunately fantastic at avoiding them. Inevitably, he managed to grab my arm and pull me behind his blade.

"Jamaica!" several voices cried in almost unison. Mark tensed to rush Dan, who sneered, "Another step, and her neck turns red!"

Pain to Match Pain

7

Even in my terrified state, only one thought crossed my mind. I am getting way too good at getting caught. The thought didn't help me at all, and I bristled when Dan's voice suddenly trickled into my head.

Your dragon can't help you now.

Don't bet on it.

Enraged, Mugireti roared, something thunderous enough to leave your very skeleton jarred. The agent's grip on his weapon tightened, but it was no use. Three large tremors sent us all to the ground. As the rest of the group dismounted and came to help, Dan stabbed the knife right in front of my throat, assuring, "You're not going anywhere."

"We've been through this before, *Dan*," Trace addressed. His voice strained to stay even, "You do anything to her, and you won't leave here alive."

I heard Dan's smirk just before a shockwave of pain racketed through my skull. I cried out, curling up and trying to hold my head. Dan grasped my wrists and sent another wave through. Mark lost any patience he had and shot a whirlwind right into the agent and me. We went tumbling, and I quickly formed a bubble around me, so the knife couldn't cause damage. As soon as we rolled to a stop, I squirmed free, running back to my group. Mark and Trace both waved me behind them, ready to attack. Trace inquired, "Are you okay?"

I shakily nodded. Dan hauled himself up, a deranged grin peeling back his lips. "Arrogant- little- twerp. Is that- all you got?"

"Get back over here and you'll find out," Mark shouted. I caught my cousin's shoulder just as he began to barge toward the agent, murmuring, "Mark, don't!"

"Jamaica-"

"We're not killers," I blurted, remembering Ed having said it. I noticed the hand on his sword hilt ease a little. He replied, "We can't just let him go."

"Why not?" he looked at me like I was crazy, and I edited, "He's dangerous, I know, but we can't kill him, and there's no reason to take him with us."

He glanced away, his lungs breathing being the only movement from him. I tried to inhale courage as I stepped past him and Trace. Dan stood there, knife still prepared, though it was clear Mark's blast had taken some fight out of him. I lifted my chin, confronting him, "Leave now. Take your team back to the OAD, and we won't hurt you."

"You? Hurt me?" Dry chortling rasped out of him, "You won't do that."

Another wave hit me, this one making me nauseous. But I could feel his footsteps coming toward me. I blindly pulled my dagger from its sheath, swung-

As I came back to focus, my stomach felt like it flopped out of my belly. My weapon had slashed him square across the chest, and I felt my breathing shut down as I saw the blood on my hand. I was aware of the warm droplets on my face too, and I couldn't shutter. His weight slumped to the side of me. I trembled, dagger dropping to the dirt. I had- I'd just-

Someone took my shoulders and turned me away, whispering, "Don't look. It'll scare you more."

Garrett. That was Garrett. That was his voice, his hands leading me away from the scene. He calmly ordered, "Sit here."

I lowered onto a log, and he continued, "Hold your breath."

Water covered my face to wash off the blood. Whether it was the lack of oxygen, or the cool feeling on my skin, my brain went into overload. The water fell away, and I was gasping, freaking out, the only thought being what I'd just done-

"Hey, hey, hey," my mentor pried my hands away from my temples gently, holding them with care, "It's alright. I know you're scared, I know you're shocked-"

"I- but I-" I blubbered through the words, numbness going away all too swiftly. Garrett cut me off with another, "I know."

It was so full of knowing, and understanding, and sympathy. I watched his lips press together in worry, and the tears streamed down my cheeks out of nowhere. I reached out, and he gladly met the gesture, wrapping his arms around me, comforting, "You're alright. You're alright, Ani- Jamaica. It's okay."

----0----

The group decided to set up camp, seeing as the other agents had neither left, nor come to get their partner. Mugireti shifted the body out to the woods, not even caring where it went. Garrett had cleaned the rest of the blood off, and he became the only one I could respond to. I'd-I'd killed somebody. Forget that it

51

was an agent who easily would've taken my life, I had *killed* him. The thought was sickening, and I had almost thrown up several times. I didn't eat dinner. I wasn't hungry, and I doubted I could keep it down anyway.

"Jamaica," someone softly pleaded as he knelt in front of me. I recognized the hands speckled with scars before I even saw the dark blue eyes. "Garrett told me not to get too close. Said I might scare you. But…"

The ocean eyes drifted away. "It wasn't…you weren't…it was self-defense. He was attacking, you were reacting, you couldn't control the situation-"

"I said you could talk to her if ya didn't bring it up," Garrett's voice scolded behind me. I realized a tear was strolling down my cheek. Trace insisted, "She needs to know it wasn't her fault-"

"And she will, with time. But it ain't any a' your business tryin' to convince her when it just happened." Trace's fingers played around a little before, "Then I'll stay off the subject."

"Boy-"

"Please," Trace begged. I heard desperation in his voice. Garrett's breath audibly heaved. "If I have to come back here, I'm draggin' ya away by the ear. Understand?"

Trace nodded, and our mentor's heavy footsteps grew faint. The boy sat on his heels in silence for a little while. "So…I know you said you're not the math whiz, but…do you know what two-point-six times one-point-four is?"

That's right. Math was his worst course in remedial. Dagger in Dan's chest. Two-point- six. Blood on my hand. Times one-point-four. Dead, killed. What was the answer? "No."

I finally reanimated, holding my head, "Don't know. Don't- no-"

"Hey," he murmured. I gasped as he risked taking my hands in his. "It's okay, I didn't expect you to answer. Just...trying to make you smile somehow."

His thumbs rubbed misshapen circles on the joints of mine. How could he...touch my hand? It had had blood on it, how could...?

His hands tensed, and I noticed him staring at them, sullen.

"You know," he swallowed, "I've had an accident or two, myself. Never intentional, but- when you're running for your life, you can't always control what happens to the chasers."

I sat listening. So, he had really...? "And then sometimes, people around you become extra losses, and you never really get the time to think about it. Or, well...I didn't, before my mom..."

He started to struggle with even breathing, hands tightening. "I didn't-didn't think-"

That's when the first choked back sob escaped him. I realized he was trembling, hunching over, trying to make himself disappear just as much as I had been wanting to turn invisible. He croaked, "I want her back. I miss her too much, I need her back."

Before I knew what I was doing, I was down on my knees, taking my hands from his and wrapping my arms over his shoulders. I still couldn't look anywhere but straight forward, but a sort of odd comfort washed over me, dulling the horror. Trace tightly hugged my midsection and rested his forehead in my neck, clearly still trying to hold back. Even still, how much trust had it taken him to let down his walls enough to talk about Mrs. Maruken? And why would he have risked that much vulnerability, knowing I might not react?

I was more than willing to stay like that forever. I had never comprehended just how comforting a hug could be from someone you...someone you cared about.

"Trace," I sighed. I said his name over and over. It rolled off the tongue so easily. For me, at least.

Eventually, all the tears he could muster had reached his chin, and his lungs started to breathe relatively normally, but he made no move to release me. The moment I began to pull back, he croaked, "Don't leave. Please."

So I melted back into him. He'd taken on the smell of the forest fast. And wanting to absorb more of that comfort, I found my grip constricting, my eyes finally able to close.

A ticking clock, slow and menacing. It was counting down limited time, reminding that the end was never far away. The color red, dark and brutal. A pool of it, swirling down a drain that was suddenly the pupil of a dark blue eye. A picture frame, with the face in the portrait blackened. The black started to fade away, a vaguely familiar face showing up-

I started awake with a gasp. It wasn't quite a nightmare. It was sort of vision-like, if not very clear.

There are some things I cannot directly show you. You have yet to see.

Courtney. That was Courtney.

Upon finding myself pinned under Trace's arm, with him fast asleep, I took his shoulder- he jumped. Light sleeper I suppose. "What, what-?"

"Sh," I commanded. In the dawning morning light, I sat up and focused.

I didn't bring the stone with me. Speak again.

There are things to pass that if I should tell you now, your journey will not progress.

Then why show them to me?

Because you must always be aware of what the future may hold.

"What the future may hold…but what does that- mean?" Her presence faded out of my head just as quickly as it had come. I muttered, "Great."

Trace had a weirded out look on his face, and a good scrape on his cheek from rubbing it on the bark of the log we'd fallen asleep on. He slowly questioned, "Everything okay?"

"Courtney is speaking in riddles." I passive-aggressively added, "And in case she doesn't know, that's not very helpful to a fourteen-year-old girl."

"Courtney," my boyfriend's brow creased in thought, "…your past life?"

I nodded, standing up to brush the dirt and moss off my clothes. "So…are you feeling any better?"

Trace was reluctant to ask, and I was reluctant to tell. "Not really. You?"

"Not really," he agreed, setting an elbow on one peaked knee, "What did Courtney show you about 'the future'?"

I sat down on the log next to him, thinking out loud, "A clock, the color red, and a picture frame. I kind of understand the first two, but the last one…you know how Mark's father died when he was a little kid?"

"Yeah," he answered, a bit hesitant. I continued, "Call me crazy, but- I could've sworn it was his face in the picture. It was blacked out, and then the black faded."

"So what does that mean?" he pressed, unsure. I wasn't too certain myself, and admitted, "I don't know. But he's been dead a long time-"

And then it clicked. "What if he's alive?"

"Going for the 'parent isn't really dead' strategy," Trace noted. I hushed, "Hear me out. Black is a common symbol for death. His face was blacked out, but the black going away-?"

"So he's gonna come back from the dead?" Trace guessed, still confused. I grabbed him by the shoulders as a tiny bit of excitement welled. "No, silly! He might not have ever died at all! Mark's dad could be alive!"

"He's dead." We both turned to see Mark standing a few feet behind me. His hands were shoved in his pockets, but it wasn't difficult to know they were balled. "Mark-"

"I saw that explosion, Jamaica. Don't try to make me believe otherwise."

"I wasn't going to-"

"I get that you have this sort of fantasy that your mom is safe and sound somehow, but don't try to stretch it!" he shot, anger and hurt coming through, "I saw what happened, I went to the funeral, I was upset for months! Don't try to go convincing people that he's alive, because I know he *isn't*!"

"Mark-"

"Stay out of it!" he snarled, raising a flaming hand in Trace's direction. I could nonetheless see Trace poising to lunge, just in case. People were starting to wake up, and I could see Will kicking Garrett. He had his eyes trained on Mark's hand. I stood, gently trying to talk him down, "Mark, it's just a stupid theory-"

"Then keep it to yourself!" I felt my body float backwards as the flames came towards me.

A Son's Memory

8

I had tripped. My heel had caught a tree root, and I had tripped. Mark's hand was splayed out in front of him, fire diminishing as he forced a cushion of air under me. And when I looked down, I saw the huge rock jutting out of the earth. My head would've conked against it if Mark hadn't stopped my fall. But the spark of fear on his face left as swift as it had appeared. "Don't spread a story that isn't true."

The cushion thinned until I was laying down, and Mark trudged away from camp. After a tense second, Anna questioned, "Okay, does *someone* want to explain what just happened?"

"Should we go after him, or-?"

"I'll go talk to him," I interrupted Scarlet. Trace grabbed my wrist, and I insisted, "I have to."

Mark hadn't gone very far. He was curled up against the back of a tree, facing the forest. "Go away, Jamaica."

"Mark-"

"He's dead," my cousin reiterated, lifting his head to look at me. But he rested on his arms again saying softer, "I watched it."

I sat down next to him, pulling my knees up.

Too bad it was only the first time.

"Jamaica, what you did wasn't on purpose. What?" I stared at him incredulously and gawked, "You heard me?"

"Yeah," he answered. He didn't realize what had happened.

You can hear this?

When he didn't see my lips move, he understood. Mark's eyes widened, and a grin spread over his face.

Yes. Can you hear me?

Yes!

Jeff, our blacksmith friend with the most knowledge on dragon and rider history, had explained that the human side of a cluster had to share a 'profound' bond before mental communication was possible. But none of the three of us had been able to make it work, until now.

Can I try something?

What is it?

I want to try and show you a memory. O-Of that night.

A memory? He wanted to show me the night of the explosion?

O-Okay. If you're up to it.

He closed his eyes and focused. I closed mine when a mental picture hazed into view.

----0----

"Mama, c'mon! ¡Rapidamente!" A little brown boy excitedly chirped. Aunt Janice walked by him, saying, "Only your father is allowed to say that to me, sweetie."

While Aunt Janice was starkly white compared to the little boy, I knew it was Mark. It had never occurred to me that Mark

58

might know Spanish from his father. He whined, "But Papa said he was gonna show me a new invention! He said it shocks people!"

"Did he?" Aunt Jan laughed, putting earrings in. Little Mark started jumping and running through the house, urging his mother to hurry. They were soon out the door and in a car with a distinct smell of- cranberries?

Papa's favorite...

Mark explained what his father had told him about the invention, or as well as a seven-year-old could. Aunt Jan just smiled as she drove down a quiet road in the dark. They soon pulled into a near empty parking lot on a hill, a lone building at the base with its lights on. "C'mon, c'mon!"

"Settle down, Mark, you're lucky I'm letting you stay up this late-"

There was a bright burst, and a loud, crackling boom. Then, a dark cloud rose over the building, orange light now glowing from inside. "Papa!"

"Mark, no-"

Aunt Jan couldn't grab him fast enough. The little boy raced down the hill, screaming for his father. Someone shoved him out of the way, knocking him to the ground. He didn't see who it was, but he was back on his feet about to run in-

"Mark!" Aunt Jan scooped him up and carried him away from the building. He was sobbing, still crying 'Papa' over and over. A secondary explosion shot more fire out of the remaining fragments of the windows and sent Aunt Jan skidding over the grass on her shoulder, holding Mark tight to her chest. A hand reached out toward his little arm-

----0----

The image went black as Mark raggedly inhaled beside me. He stared forward in horror, whispering, "Papa."

59

The horror melted into tears that my cousin tried to hold back, burying his face in his arms. I wasn't entirely sure what to do. I had just seen what he saw that night. The explosion, the fire, his mom taking him away from it all-

"Mark...I know I shouldn't prod you on any further, but- who reached out for you?" It took a moment before he mumbled, "I don't know."

Without my asking, he closed his eyes to look again, and shared his search with me. The image was much fuzzier this time, like a TV with a channel full of static.

----0----

The hand was there, frozen. And then Mark was standing, the hand grasping his arm. Aunt Jan was standing too, a small thing of pepper spray held out towards someone on Mark's right. "It may not be your fancy sword, but it will send you howling!"

Mark was now behind his mother's leg, peering out at two men. One with an OAD uniform, the other with cat green eyes. The Emperor smiled at him, and Mark hid. Izoles' voice drifted, "We have what we came for."

----0----

"No more," Mark gasped, eyes screwed tight. "I don't remember anything else, it's all black until the fire department arrived, and then I went back to crying."

"It's okay, I won't make you try to remember anything else," I assured, touching his shoulder lightly. He panted, "How could I not remember that? How could I not remember seeing him, knowing he was there-?"

"You were seven, Mark, you were in shock-"

"Jamaica, he caused it!" Mark panicked, "He's the reason my dad was-was…"

His brain stopped forming words as he relived his own shock. "Mark. Mark."

I stopped, thinking about what Garrett said. "Don't think about it. It'll make it worse."

"What am I supposed to be thinking about, J? I can't just turn it off like a switch," he murmured, though it seemed to reel him in a little. I scoured for an answer to give him, and finally blurted, "Why does he call himself 'The Emperor'? It seems so silly, doesn't it?"

I tried to smile, but it faded quickly as I looked away. The comment hadn't helped. "It's a symbol of power."

I gazed at Mark again. His eyes were still staring out, but they were more blank now. He continued, "It's the same as if he called himself King, or President. He's giving himself a level of power. The Emperor is just a name."

He licked his lips. "And I refuse to call him that any longer."

Mark's hand began to flex. His features settled into a determination that only he could possess. "I'm not going to give him that power. None of us should."

"So, what? We just call him Izoles?"

"Why not?" he reasoned, "It's his real name, isn't it?"

A Peculiar Child

9

Bruno had been watching the boy. Learning his movements, his mannerisms. How could a kid like him be an agent? He knew James had serious problems, but to force a child to do his bidding…?

It had been three days. The forest line had ended, giving way to a meadow where the helicopter landed. In the dancing firelight, the grass calmly swayed in a night breeze.

The boy's older partner stared at Bruno in a way that was almost unnerving. Sure, he was on watch, but the eye contact was only ever broken when the man blinked.

"Would you stop staring at him like that? You're creeping me out," the boy huffed, tossing a sleeping bag at the man, who only replied, "I'll stop staring at him when he stops staring at me."

The boy's gaze transferred to Bruno. Had it been obvious that he was observing through the slits between his eyelids? "He's asleep, you nitwit. Stop being paranoid."

"You should be more paranoid, kid. You of all people know the Emperor's got something in store for him, and I'll betcha he knows it too."

"It doesn't concern us," the boy replied, reserved. But the man only asked, "What would he want with this guy, anyway? He's a blacksmith. What's he gonna do, take inventory of the armory?"

"It's his brother," the boy answered softer. The older agent continued, "You think he knows? Maybe he helps the boss-"

"He doesn't," the boy shot, something resembling defensiveness in his voice, "He works for the riders. Now, shut up and go to sleep. I'll take watch tonight."

"Ah c'mon, let's wake him up and see what he knows. We could learn something interesting about 'the Emperor.'" The man got up and started to saunter over. Bruno fought to keep his muscles relaxed and breath steady.

"Cortez-"

"What? He'll probably crack open and spill everything with a few good threats-" the younger got to his feet and shoved his partner back just feet away from Bruno. Then, the boy drew a sword from the sheathe on his hip. Bruno had noticed the weapon before, but never truly acknowledged its presence before now.

"If you touch him, you're going to be sorry," the boy growled. The older held up his hands, bristling, "Hey, hey! Take it easy-!"

"We have a half a day of flying left. If we get him there *unharmed*, we get to move on with the pathetic excuses of our lives. I, for one, don't want my head lobbed off!" The boy hissed. The other agent deflected, "He wouldn't kill you, you're-"

"It doesn't matter!" the boy snarled, grip on the hilt visibly tightening, "He's a cruel man in many ways to many people. I'm no exception!"

Bruno heard the slight waver in the last sentence. His brow inched together ever so slightly.

"He wouldn't kill you," The older repeated, more firmness to his tone, "Even he isn't that low. Remember who you are to him, kid."

"He doesn't care who I am," the boy's voice shook with anger, but he lowered his weapon and put it away after a moment, "I'm just another soldier to him. Now go rest before I knock you out. I can't have a pilot falling asleep at the controls tomorrow."

The adult almost looked concerned as he shuffled off. The boy looked back at Bruno. Something about him was so dreadfully familiar, it was gnawing at Bruno's stomach. The young agent closed the small distance between them. He would've been staring dead into Bruno's eyes if they weren't almost closed.

"If you're going to pretend to be asleep," Bruno heard softly, "at least breathe evenly…you sound ridiculous."

And the boy went to take watch. An inkling of who he resembled trickled into Bruno's mind, but he was quick to block it. This kid couldn't be…

----0----

A boot kicked Bruno's thigh, and he started. He'd fallen asleep at some point, probably not long after the fight. "Wake up."

That boy again. The blacksmith felt a hand grab his arm, helping him to his feet and then prodding him toward the helicopter. The pilot was already up, doing the last of his checks and procedures for flying. The boy buckled Bruno, then himself into the back seats. The copter lifted from the ground, and Bruno's stomach churned. The last thing he wanted was to see James again.

He looked over at the boy next to him. What had James done to convince him? More likely, what had James used to blackmail him? "Stop staring at me."

64

Bruno blinked. He had completely tuned out in his own brief thoughts. And in coming back, he almost downright asked who the boy was. That would be a bad move. Bruno released the air in his lungs and looked away. The rhythm of the rotor blades stirred his organs into one of Andrew's stews.

It only got worse when, several hours later, a building from his oldest memories appeared on the horizon, along with a rocky climb leading toward it. He couldn't help shifting uneasily. Bruno hadn't seen the facility since he was young. And after James took over, he'd never wanted to see it again.

The helicopter neared it in minutes, hovering down until it made contact with a landing pad. Hands immediately reached in ahead of bodies, ripping Bruno from his seat and just about slamming him into solid ground. He was pulled, and shoved, and tossed around until two pairs of hands finally latched onto his arms, hauling him out of the crowd. But before he could grab his bearings, his knees hit red carpet. Bruno was panting, somehow out of breath. Was that the taste of blood? Had he split his lip-?

"Well, well, little brother. It's been quite some time, hasn't it?" Bruno pursed his lips and cautiously looked up at James as he approached. The older brother cooed, "What? All these years, and you don't have so much as a greeting for me? No words to express your disdain?"

On the contrary, Bruno had plenty of words to express much more than disdain. But he wouldn't let his tongue fly. He would lose his temper and be no better than the man before him. Seeing this very clearly, James' gaze moved to the boy. He had slipped into the room behind Bruno without a sound. "What do you have to report?"

"The outcome was optimal, Sir. We had no interference from the riders, and no objection from the target." The blacksmith felt a pang of sympathy. Under this boy's calmness, his voice quivered ever so slightly, and it was enough to tell the truth. This child was petrified. "May I request-? Sir."

James' expression was expectant as the boy hesitantly continued, "I-I would like to retire to- *her* quarters. If you will permit."

James became amused, but only replied, "You completed your assignment with satisfactory results. You are dismissed."

The young agent cautiously slipped past him and made a beeline off to the other end of the room. James and Bruno both watched as he disappeared around a hidden corner.

"Who is he, James?" Bruno murmured. He couldn't hold the urge back any longer, he had to know. "Surely you know, little brother-"

"Don't play games," Bruno scolded, "Who is he?"

James laughed. He actually *laughed*. The sound made him seem so human. But for Bruno, it was like getting slapped across the face, something more familiar to him than it should've been.

As the older brother settled, he joked, "Are your observational skills lacking so much that you cannot see it? Or are you in denial of what you have seen?"

James was suddenly crouching in front of him, and Bruno bit back the desire to lunge. The elder's youthful face was curled into a sneer. Bruno wondered what he would look like at his true age. "Ah, denial. Well set your doubt aside, little brother. It is him."

"He is a child, James," Bruno protested, "It is inhumane to thrust this life on the boy-"

"But you see, I haven't," Bruno's stomach churned as the sneer grew, "He chose it for himself."

The blacksmith knew his face had slacked. He knew shock was written into his features. He couldn't help it. All Bruno could do was try to process it as the guards heaved him up and prodded him out the doors, across the facility, and eventually, into a cell.

The cell door slammed, so did the outside door, and he still couldn't wrap his head around it. What had James done to him? That innocent little newborn from so long ago...

Bruno pressed the heels of his palms against his eyes and sighed, "Westyn."

A Strange Act of Heroism

10

Weary looks met Mark and me as we walked back to camp. If anyone had still been asleep when he yelled, they were up now. Anna walked up to us, arms folded, while everyone watched. "You cool?"

"Icy," he replied with a snarky tone. I wasn't accustomed to that coming from him. I glanced between the two as Anna's eyes narrowed. A shrill whistle caught our attention as Garrett called, "Let's get movin'. We gotta get Bruno, too."

Everyone swarmed toward their designated dragon, whether rider or passenger. I had just circled around Mugireti to climb up when I heard the whisper, "Jamaica."

My dragon just about impaled Ed with his teeth as I backed away from the trees he was hiding behind. Just before I screamed, he frantically continued, "Sh, sh! I'm not here to hurt you. Just listen to me for a few seconds, alright? Dan is on his second life now, you need to be careful-"

Trace appeared, eyes widening as he saw the agent, cautiously saying, "Jamaica?"

"I didn't plan this-"

"Jamaica, Trace! Get your hustle on, we're all waitin' on you!" Garrett called. I watched several emotions cross Ed's face, from surprise and anticipation, to sadness and longing. His features hardened as he finished, "Heed my warning. Tell the others so he can't surprise you. Please."

"Jamaica, c'mon," Trace murmured. He had climbed to Mugireti's spine and was holding a hand down. I looked back at the trees, but Ed was gone. I turned and used Mugireti's talon as a stepping stool, denying Trace's offer. "If you try to use your muscles before those cuts heal, you could cause more damage."

What did he say?

Something about Dan being on his second life.

You two seem awfully calm for having been confronted by an agent.

She thinks he's trustworthy.

As Mugireti spread his wings and took to the sky, I shot Trace a glare. Because of him, I was about to get a lecture.

Jamaica, he works for the Emperor-

Something's different about him, though! Whatever he means about Dan, he's clearly trying to help us!

He's probably trying to scare you.

While I don't trust him, Jamaica is right that he's helped us a couple times already. Maybe he's telling the truth.

The man is dead. No amount of saying so will bring him back, and that is most certainly for the best.

With that, Mugireti cut the conversation short.

Hey, Jamaica?

Trace, don't get me in trouble again.

What if the agents try to get us back? I'll take your word about Ed, even if Mugireti doesn't, but Cory and Fernando could retaliate. And they have to come back this way anyway so they can return to headquarters.

I hadn't thought about that.

They never came looking. Maybe they hated him as much as we did.

Mm.

His arms held my waist a little tighter, causing me to duck my head down. I didn't know if I was blushing, but he certainly didn't need to find out. As the wind rushed by, I started to play that explosion from Mark's childhood through my mind.

Hey, Mark.

Out of the corner of my eye, I saw the smaller of two black dragons teeter a little.

Geez, don't scare me like that! I almost fell off!

Sorry.

What's up?

I don't know. Felt like testing the connection for distance.

There was a pause.

Liar. Jamaica, I'm fine. I've played it all through my mind a lot.

You've never had to relive it.

Another pause, longer this time.

It's painful. But it helped, in a twisted way. I know more now, I remember more. It doesn't bring my dad back, but…

I could sense him searching for a choice of words and coming up with nothing.

…it helps.

He went quiet after that, and I suppose I did, too. Most of the rides were quiet, but right now it just seemed different. Maybe I felt the need to talk to someone after- yesterday. I forced myself away from the memory. I wasn't ready to review it yet.

----0----

Mugireti, stop looking behind you! You're going to bank right into Mescheaf!

You don't sense that? The vibrations?

He wasn't wrong. A faint resonance disturbed the air, and by the size of the disruption, it could only mean one thing.

The agents are following us, aren't they?

It would appear so. We should land, before they can get close.

I agreed, so he sent out the message, and the dragons were quick to slow down and slip into the forest. The sky was turning into a sunset, so we would have had to land soon anyway. Trace's feet hit the ground first, and he helped me down.

I noticed K.C. biting her lip as she talked to Kaia, and Garrett rubbing Mescheaf's cheek as he leaned his hand loosely on the hilt of his knife. Both actions were respective signs of nerves, I had learned, and I had no doubt everyone else showed similar signs. Trace set a hand on my shoulder, trying to ease my constricting muscles.

I caught sight of Will's beckoning hand and strode over, Mark and K.C. close behind me. Will was already pacing by the time we reached him and Garrett, who had moved to prop himself up against Mescheaf's foreleg. The oldest rider cleared his throat, grumbling, "So, bein' I was the only one not feelin' 'vibrations,' one of ya wanna fill me in?"

He glanced over at his partner. "Will."

The man stopped abruptly. "Sorry. The vibrations are the agents' helicopter."

And his hands began to move, almost absentmindedly playing with fire. I asked, "Are you okay?"

"Agents make him anxious. Anxiety makes him fidgety," Garrett explained, "He's been like that since eleven or twelve."

71

"Shut up," Will snipped, though he looked at no one, and only seemed to prove Garrett's point. K.C. worried, "If we know they're coming, what are we going to do? Hide and let them fly over-?"

"No," Will cut her off, "They'll be landing soon."

My cousins all gave him confused looks, and when he finally noticed, he put shortly, "Connect your senses to your powers. You can do more than just feel things."

"Ah, so you're listenin' to their conversation," Garrett guessed. Will nodded, returning to his pacing. Us kids shifted our expressions to the elder, who calmly clarified, "Like Jamaica usin' roots to extend her sense a' touch, he uses the air to extend his hearin' to listen for conversation between the agents. What're they sayin'?"

"Planning," Will mumbled, spinning on heel for at least the twentieth time, "Going home empty isn't an option…can't risk anymore…Jamaica."

He stopped, looking straight at me. "They're after Jamaica again. And they're willing to take bait if they need to."

"We need everyone to lay low. Hide them under the dragons' wings maybe," Mark suggested, "We can take the agents."

Garrett swallowed, folding his arms. "I'd rather you kids not get involved."

"They got us involved," Mark argued, "We wouldn't be a part of this if they didn't strike first."

Garrett's gaze transferred to me, and I could only shrug, "He does have a point."

He sighed, dragging a hand down his face. "Sometimes I wonder if you kids like gettin' yourselves into trouble."

Through his accent, we could all hear annoyance, but a good amount of concern along with it. Mark pressed, "Should we go then? Get the drop on them?"

Garrett pushed off his dragon's leg and approached Mr. Maruken, explaining the situation and likely putting him in charge. Trace, who had been observing the situation, traded glances with Mugireti.

The oldest rider made his way back to us, capturing Will's attention before nodding, "Alright. Let's go."

The five of us slipped further into the trees, away from safety. Garrett muttered, "Jamaica, can ya give us a direction?"

I knelt down, flattening my hand over the soil. Allowing the trees' root systems to spread my senses for me, I found the helicopter grounded just over a mile away. But the agents had already started walking toward us, a good distance closer than the helicopter. I brought my senses back, sucking in a breath. "Helicopter's about a mile away, but they're walking our direction. That way."

I stood and pointed in the direction we had flown from.

Jamaica, what are you doing?

My dad said the riders would be gone for a few minutes.

Guys, it'll be fine. We have Garrett and Will with us.

That was hardly a good enough excuse to give my boyfriend and dragon, but I got the feeling Garrett didn't want us spreading word of the plan. We crept at a swift pace, me checking through trees here and there to see how close our opponents were. When they were almost within visual range, I commanded, "Get down!"

Everyone dropped into the underbrush, hands ready to grab weapons. A moment later, three bodies appeared. I quickly realized Ed was missing, and with sickening relief, that Dan was alive. And then I comprehended that Mark had prematurely drawn his sword and gone running. Will threw his hand to the side, sending Mark soaring out of harm's way and skidding off into the underbrush in the sidelines. But the agents were alert now, looking for the rest of us. Dan ordered, "Go get him-"

73

A wind wall zigzagged through trees, cutting the agents off from him. Garrett growled, "Will-"

"K.C., we need to make sure he's not hurt," Will instructed, ignoring his partner. Both got up and sprinted towards where he landed. The wall soon turned into a pillar, A hazy picture inside of K.C. disappearing behind bushes while Will held up his hands to stabilize the wind.

"Damn it, Will," Garrett hissed, watching Fernando and Cory head to the pillar at Dan's order. "Jamaica, stay here and *don't move*."

I complied more than willingly, and before Garrett even rose, Dan yelled, "Come out, come out! I know there's more of you!"

Garrett slowly stood, making absolutely sure he could be seen before stalking towards the oldest of the agents. An ugly smile curled across Dan's face. The rider stopped just in front of him, growling through his teeth, "Go on, then."

Dan ripped out a knife, Garrett blocked it with his own and punched him low in the stomach. Dan hunched over and stumbled back, but Garrett wasn't about to let him have that space. He closed the distance and cocked his elbow for another swing-

Dan moved fast, head butting him in the chest. Both staggered, and Dan attacked again, throwing a fist across Garrett's temple before the man could get his breath back. Garrett fell like a tree, collapsing on his stomach. I screamed, "GARRETT!!"

He wasn't moving. Why wasn't he moving-?! An agent, Fernando, was hoisting me to my feet, holding me back. The wind pillar had destabilized, and Cory had reached through, quickly subduing Will, despite several bursts of fire. I watched in horror as Dan kicked my mentor's shoulder up with his toe and shoved it over with his heel, sending Garrett onto his back. The rider coughed a little, signaling that he was still alive, but too dazed to move. I pulled frantically against Fernando's hands, crying, "No! Leave him alone!"

Dan smirked, "And the Emperor said he was a strong one. Let's get him out of the way, then, if he's such a threat-"

"Get away from him!" Ed seemingly appeared out of nowhere, pushing Dan away from Garrett and standing over the rider. Dan bared his teeth. "You call yourself one of us, but you keep helping them! The hell's wrong with you-?!"

"I will beg on my knees if I have to. Don't hurt him." Ed had his hands out in a defensive stance. All the rest of us could do was watch the scene play out. Dan snarled, "He's a rider!"

"He's-!" Ed sputtered, and for some reason, I found myself hanging onto his words. What had he been about to say? "Please. You don't have to do this. Don't do it. Please, not to him."

Dan scowled deeply, and suddenly, he barged over to me, tearing my arms from Fernando. He put me in a one-armed headlock and held his knife up to my neck. Will struggled against Cory, but still no use. Ed had turned, and I could see his eyes rimmed red as he protested, "Dan, he'll kill us all-!"

"Fine!" the man spat, "I'm tired of listening to you whine and piss about leaving these brats alone when any one of them could kill u-uh...uh..."

My heart just about stopped. A sword blade had pierced through his chest, narrowly missing my shoulder, blood spurting out. He fell forward, taking me with him. If I hadn't caught myself, who knows where the agent's knife would have landed.

I freaked as someone grabbed my arm again, but it was Mark helping me up, having abandoned his weapon in Dan's back. One hand was lit and pointed at Fernando, keeping him from restraining either of us. My cousin shouted with pride, "If you want to kill her, or anyone else on this team, you have to go through me first!"

Flames consumed his arm the moment Fernando moved to take him.

"Try it," Mark challenged, "I dare you."

"Let him go, Cory," Ed numbly demanded. When Cory disagreed, Ed roared, "LET HIM GO!!"

Cory's hands popped right off Will's arms, and the rider's first reaction was to pull his machete out to defend K.C. Ed shakily dealt, "You take your man. We take ours. We'll leave you alone."

"Promi-"

"Swear," Ed intervened, looking Mark dead in the eyes. He looked down at the older rider under him, and everyone could see the fists curling up as he tried to maintain self-control. "Keep him safe. That's all I ask. Please."

When Mark was hesitant to answer, I spoke up, "We will. I swear."

After a second, he bobbed his head, forcing his hands to relax. He backed away, and Will was at Garrett's side in a heartbeat, calling Mark to help him. Ed waved Cory over to help Fernando, and I tripped over my feet stepping back as they went to lift Dan's body. I looked over to where a small bit of red hair was visible, and went over to get K.C. She was crouched low, watching through the bushes. Her eyes could've been the size of shrimp platters for all I cared. Ed had protected our mentor. Nearly got me killed in the process, but he was ready to die for Garrett. And I still didn't understand why.

----0----

You what?!

Mugireti-

No! No Mugireti-ing me! Jamaica, that was reckless! No, that was beyond reckless! It was stupid! You almost got killed!

Not for the first time on this trip.

His muzzle shoved me backwards.

Don't you dare. *I have been worried sick over you this whole trip for that very reason! Don't say it like it's just- some- other-*

He shoved me again, knocking me to the ground. I saw how upset he was and comprehended the worst part. I could do nothing about it.

I watched him lumber away to go lay down by himself, back to the rest of the group. "Looks like you ticked him off pretty well."

I looked up at Trace, hands stuffed in his pockets, gazing at my dragon. I started to get up. "It wasn't the plan."

"Well, if you hadn't gone off for the agents-"

"Why are you two treating it like I did this all by myself?!" I cracked, "I was with Mark and K.C.! With Will and Garrett-!"

"And look what happened," he calmly retorted. I knew what he was referring to. Garrett had regained some of his bearings soon after we returned to camp, but he was still disoriented, to the point that he was only allowed to rest. Will had stayed with him while Mark checked on K.C. And I had been reproached by my dragon. Trace continued, "Garrett is a great rider, and a great fighter, but he's not what he used to be. We all know that."

"Dan wasn't much younger-"

"Dan took him out with two hits-"

"Dan is dead." He just glanced at me, and back at Mugireti. "There are other agents like him. That's why Mugireti is so worried. He couldn't protect you from Dan. He's terrified of someone else coming along."

"So, what? He doesn't trust me to take care of myself?"

"It's not that," Trace shook his head, "He thinks you don't trust him enough to keep you safe."

"What?" I balked, "Of course I do! He's my dragon, I don't trust anyone more than him!"

77

"Then why didn't you tell him where you were going?" my boyfriend pointed out, to my distaste. I could say that Garrett didn't want us to, but I had a feeling that would only make it worse. I cautiously walked toward Mugireti.

Go. Away.

He curled his tail and neck in tighter, wings squeezing closed even more. I bit the inside of my cheek and apologized, "I was wrong to not tell you. I thought with five riders we were going to be okay, and things went bad really fast. I should've asked for your help."

He didn't move, so I carefully walked around his front, over to his stomach. He looked away when I knelt down and touched his cheek. It was wet, and a fresh stream trickled down from the corner of his eye. "Mugireti…"

How can I be your protector when I don't even know where you are?

"I'm sorry," I mumbled, stroking the hard ridge above his eye, "I'm so, so sorry, Mugireti."

Hesitantly, I reached my left arm, the one with his initial permanently scarred on the inside of my wrist, down to the tip of his nose. I settled my palm there, our emotions mixing with each other's. I felt his hurt for my seemingly lack of trust, his utter terror for my life. He felt my sincere guilt for causing him such trouble.

I promise, I'll tell you everything from now on. As my dragon, you have every right to know.

My rider.

His head shifted up, pressing into me vertically so I could hug his whole muzzle. And we stayed like that for a while, our bond strengthening just a little more in our comfort.

It Wasn't Part of the Plan

11

After a long time spent with Mugireti, I went over to check on Garrett. He was sitting up now, leaning back against Mescheaf's belly. A swollen, blackened mark had formed by his left eye, stretching up into his brow and down over his cheekbone. That hit had really done damage, and anyone could see that his dragon was ready to do any necessary harm to anyone else who wanted to throw a punch his way.

Garrett was keeping her calm, rubbing between her eye ridges, but the dragon's eyes would not stop surveying. "Did he-have any-?"

My mentor held the side of his head. He was still having trouble forming a full sentence fluidly. "Do you know his- name?"

Yes. "No. He looked young, twenties at most. For an agent, he's actually been really helpful over the past few days."

His look was still troubled, so I asked, "You don't...*know* him, do you?"

Though it was clear he was thinking something else, Garrett slowly shook his head, muttering, "No."

I decided not to press him. There was no way I would get him to talk, anyway. "Get some- sleep. We'll reach the- OAD tomorrow."

He patted my thigh once, then twice, forcing down a scowl as he closed his eyes and let his head fall back onto Mescheaf. The dragon flicked her eyes with a flash of sympathy, so I got up and left. As I made my way back to Mugireti, I noticed Mark sitting by the center fire, playing with the flames. It wasn't abnormal of him, but his body didn't seem as relaxed. And I s'pose I knew why.

He looked over as I sat down next to him. "Hey."

"Hey," he returned, looking back at the fire. I fought myself for a moment before sighing, "About Dan-"

"It's not the first time." I stopped, and given a pause, he continued, "I've had blood on my sword before, and not because I was stupid and got myself by accident. Our trip last year…"

As he shakily recalled that night, it came back to me. I'd been tired at the time, but I remembered seeing the devil hound, and Mark protecting an injured Trace from it. Remembered seeing it go limp. Mark was visibly struggling to keep under control by the time he finished talking, and unintentionally made the fire pop like it would explode at any moment. "Mark."

"I thought it would be easier. I thought if I'd already done it once, I could do it again, even to someone who deserved it anyway. But I still feel- *disgusted*."

"You acted out of defense." He licked his lips. "So then what happens the first time I act on offense?"

Well, I didn't have an answer for that. So I knocked his shoulder, smiling, "Then, I'll be there when you need me."

He granted me half a smile and knocked me back. "Thanks."

Neither of our smiles had been all that genuine, but I figured if he at least knew someone with the same experience was there to talk, it could help just a bit. We sat a little while longer before he said goodnight and went to sleep with Beuti.

Jamaica, c'mon. You need your rest for tomorrow.
Coming.

I don't know why I brushed myself off when I got up. I would be back on the ground in seconds. And as I plopped down against him, I got to thinking.

They never took off.
I know.
I'm staying awake-
Oh no you're not. You are going to sleep. You've had too much excitement today, and I can see that it's wearing you out.
But-

His head rose to eye level.

Sleep.

And he rested it again. I groaned in annoyance but lay down and let his wing slide over me. It didn't take me long to pass out, but sure enough, my sleep was not about to be peaceful.

----0----

Panic. It swam through my veins, filled my lungs and controlled my thoughts. Trace was covered in a red spot on his shirt that only continued to grow with the pool under him. He was staring up at the sky, unmoving. A battle raged, but he remained untouched.

I woke up then, sitting straight as a nail. Mugireti's face was in front of me, eyes filled with worry.

Are you alright?
I'm fine.

81

Another nightmare-?

I said I'm fine!

Mugireti was taken back at the snap.

Jamaica, if something's wrong, tell me.

It's nothing-

We stopped at the sound of cracking twigs.

Mugireti, who's out there?

We both snuck a peek out of his wing to see a small figure darting away into the woods.

Jamaica-

I was already racing out after the person. Had one of the agents snuck into camp? Ed maybe? No, the figure was too short, the frame too slim. In fact, it really looked like-

She turned with a throwing knife in hand, and being so close behind her already, the blade cut the side of my upper left arm. I grasped my arm and came to my knees, trying to hold back cries of pain. "Jamie, it's me!"

She stopped, tousled light blonde hair reflecting the moonlight that got through the canopy. "Jamaica? Jamaica, I'm so sorry, I thought you were someone else."

She knelt down next to me, hesitantly reaching out for my arm. "If I'd known it was you, I swear-"

"What are you doing out here?" I pushed through my teeth, trying to cover as much of the cut as I could with my hand. She explained, "I-I went for a run. The psych lady that sees Trace and me says exercise can help with stress, so I decided to try it. And then, when you started chasing me, I assumed you were one of the agents, and…"

She looked at my arm again. "I screwed up, I'm sorry."

"It was an accident," I told her, "and the agents aren't going to hurt us anymore."

"How do you know?"

"Because one of them swore not to." I clutched my arm as my nerves renewed the pain. Jamie got up to go find her knife.

Mark, Trace, whichever one of you is up, wake K.C. Jamie and I had- a mishap.

I didn't even know if they had heard me, but I just called back to Jamie, "Let's head back to camp, get my arm fixed up-"

The moment I uncovered the cut to look, a sudden new shot of agony went up my arm as a knife appeared in the tree in front of her. There was now a bloody 'X' on my arm as a scarily familiar voice sneered, "I don't think so."

I forced my hand back over the cuts, even though it made me cringe, and looked around until I found the faces of Cory and Fernando. Cory had a second knife in hand, while Fernando stood behind him uncertainly. Jamie raced up behind me, her own small knife reclaimed.

"C'mon, don't tell me that little scrape is all it took," Cory delighted, "The all-powerful rider should be stronger than that."

Jamie started to reach for another of her weapons, but I stopped her.

Mark. Trace. Mugireti? Someone, please.

"You want her, you go through me!" Jamie yelled proudly, striding forward to protect me. I hissed, "Jamie be quiet!"

"I've got no problem with that," Cory answered, cracking his knuckles. Fernando mumbled, "Cory, maybe we shouldn't-"

The ground shook, and there were black and white wings suddenly blocking my view. Jamie and I looked around, baffled a moment before realizing it was Beuti. Seconds later, Mark slipped under her wings from behind. "*This* is what you call a mishap?"

"That's what it was before they showed up!" I protested. Cory shouted, "Get out here, runt! That dragon can't protect you forever!"

Mugireti...

"Runt?" Mark inquired. I shrugged my shoulders, so he shouted, "Over my dead body!"

"Shit," the man cursed under his breath. Mark knelt down next to me, saying, "We need to get back to camp. Where we're safer-"

"Ah!" I gasped as he snatched my arm. That was the point he understood that blood was trickling down my skin. His expression grew darker than the nighttime forest. "What happened?"

"I'll explain later." I desperately replied. It was enough that he stood as Jamie helped me up, whispering, "On the count of three, slip behind Beuti and run for your life. One, two-"

Beuti sent a jet of fire flying, and a string of profanity rang out. Jamie finished, "Three!"

We bolted, blindly running through the trees. My foot caught on something, and I went down hard on my arm. Mark gently pulled me up, encouraging, "Come on, Jamaica, you can do it. Just a little further."

We kept going, Jamie keeping up with us, but just on the perimeter of camp, I tripped again. Mark sat me up just as K.C. and Trace came running. "Are you okay-?"

"She'll be fine-"

"It was an accident-"

"Alright, outta the way, move it." K.C. plunked down next to me, letting a small wave crash over my arm. Mugireti was right behind her, a strip of mineral gauze creating itself out of the surrounding plants and soil.

Correct me if I'm wrong, but didn't we just talk about this?

"Sorry, Mugireti," I apologized, "And sorry for snapping at you. It was heat of the moment stress."

I was the only one to catch the smirk on Mark's face, but the moment he started humming "Heat of the Moment" by Asia, K.C. elbowed him, grumbling, "Don't you dare."

Mark and I giggled a little just before another painful vibration went down my arm. The mineral gauze proceeded to wrap around the wounded area, helping to hold the cuts closed and clot the blood.

Tell them all to go to bed. I'll stay up with you to ensure your blood doesn't spill out in the remainder of the night.

I relayed the message, so Jamie and K.C. got up to say their goodnights, Trace squeezing my hand before leaving with them. But Mark stayed. "Mark, you need rest, too-"

"What. Happened?" he demanded. And he made it crystal clear he wouldn't leave until he got an answer. I huffed, "I woke up from-"

I glanced at my dragon, "-a nightmare, then Mugireti and I saw someone running out of camp. I followed, saw it was Jamie-"

"What happened to your arm, Jamaica?"

"If you would let me continue," I scowled, "Jamie thought I was an agent, so she used one of her knives. *That* was the mishap. Then Fernando and Cory showed up, and Cory nailed my arm a second time. Then you and Beuti came to the rescue."

"We shouldn't have trusted that stupid agent to keep his word," he glowered, but I quickly argued, "He wasn't there. He might not even know-"

"There's only three of them now, how could he not know, Jamaica?"

"Don't ask me!"

"You suggested it!"

Garrett...

"Garrett? What about him?" I looked at my cousin, surprised. I hadn't meant to share the thought. So I told him about what Ed had done to assist Trace and me, and then how Garrett kept trying to get information on the agent who had defended him. "You think he might know- and be *friendly* with- an agent?"

"It's farfetched, I know, but-"

85

"Yeah, it is. Looks like you need sleep even more than me. Goodnight."

"Mark-"

"Goodnight, J." He pushed himself up and walked back to where Beuti had just landed.

Well, that was...rude.

Let him close his eyes a little longer. It could just be exhaustion.

Hmph.

I laid down, curling into Mugireti's belly scales once more, hopefully to get a recharge.

Jamaica? What was that nightmare about?

I didn't want to think about the scene again, so I decided to be frank.

Death.

Silence.

Was it...was it a vision?

I hope not.

"Jamaica. C'mon, you're okay." I heard someone say. I felt a hand pat my cheek, so I reached up to bat it away. However, they stopped the moment I moved.

"Well, she's alive." My eyelids fluttered open to see daylight filtering down through tree leaves. I sat up, rubbing sleep out of my eyes. My cousins, Trace, and Anna all sat around me, K.C. unwrapping my arm.

"How ya feeling?" Trace asked, though it was clear he already knew the answer. I pursed my lips in a smile, and then clenched them together as K.C. doused the exposed cuts. I instinctively reached to clutch my arm, but she caught my wrist without breaking concentration.

"Don't touch, Jamaica," K.C. commanded, "can't have it infected."

"Nice to know," I grunted, hunching over, "You could've warned me first."

"I could have," she agreed, "but I figured the end result was more important. Mugireti, if you would?"

A fresh strip of mineral gauze dropped into her raised hand, and she quickly wrapped my arm once more. I gingerly squeezed it to get my blood circulation going again. "Thanks."

"No problem. Trace, your turn," K.C. smiled. He held his hands up, saying, "No, no, I'm good."

"Trace, c'mon, you need your injuries cleaned, too."

"Yeah, but-"

"Let's get to it. Shirt off, wrap off," K.C. ordered. At Trace's weird look, Mark snorted and leaned back against the nearest tree, crossing his arms and legs. Trace glared at him and shimmied out of his rag of a shirt. At his hesitation to the gauze, I reacted without thinking and started undoing my work. It took a few seconds before I realized everyone was staring, including Trace, who was blushing ever so slightly. K.C. shook her head while grinning like a maniac, Mark giggled behind a hand, and Anna just about died cackling. My hands retracted immediately, but K.C., struggling to keep a straight face, insisted, "Oh no, please continue."

After a moment, Trace offered, "I'll do the rest of it."

Anna was still laughing too much to breathe, but Mark rolled his eyes, though his mouth still curled up. Trace, torso now bare, self-consciously bent over. But K.C. denied, "Sit up straight, Trace. I need to make sure all of your cuts get cleaned."

"I hate you," he grumbled, rolling his shoulders back. His fists balled as a layer of water covered him from belly button to chin and elbow to elbow. "Now stay completely still."

He stiffened as the water began to move around him. "Uh...morning?"

Jamie ducked under Mugireti's neck and froze when she saw the scene. K.C. shortly explained, "Taking care of the bad stuff before we go get more of it."

"K.C.!"

"What?" she stopped momentarily, giving me a cynical glance. I lost my words, and Trace suggested through his teeth, "Just let her get it over with."

His muscles were so tense, I thought he would turn to stone. K.C. took almost another minute before deciding her work was done, and Trace was just about quivering at that point. Jamie watched with curiosity, asking, "Are you actually cleaning, or are you just trying to make my brother squirm?"

"Eh, a bit of both." Trace's eyes narrowed as he huffed. The water evaporated, and I looked away before I could embarrass myself again. Mugireti provided more gauze, and soon Trace was pulling on his tattered shirt again. A few cuts peeked over the edge of his chin, but lucky for him, they had scabbed over.

"So, I'm probably gonna get some bad looks for this," Anna warned, "but I think we should hold off on flying today."

"Let me ask you something," Mark piped up, "Exactly how insane *are* you?"

"Insane enough to give you a knuckle sandwich," my friend retorted. Mark sat up, and Anna instantly cocked her elbow back. Trace shoved himself out of the way, ignoring his wounds. We all watched the two stare each other down before Mark leaned back again. Anna steadily lowered her arm as she clarified, "Jamaica and Trace are both injured. Call me nuts, but it could be a bad omen."

"Nuts," Mark coughed. Her look of pure irritation spoke of how ready she was to kick him where it would hurt. Mark leisurely brought himself up again and chided, "Waiting another day puts Bruno at more risk. We need to get in sooner so we can get him out."

"If we go now, we're giving their injuries no chance to heal. I may not have met the Emperor, but the guy sure seems like the type to take advantage of that."

"We've had to do that before-"

"Can we at least get through the morning without fighting?" K.C. groaned. I agreed, "Yeah, what's up with you two? You've been getting at each other's throats a lot this whole trip."

"She started it."

"*I* started it?!" I cut in front of her before she could grab my cousin. Tired of the bickering, I grumbled, "Let's stay here for the night."

"Jamaica-"

"We have to think about Garrett, too. Mark, he'll deny it until the end of the world, but he needs a little more time to recover. That hit really took something out of him." His eyes drifted, and after a few seconds, he conceded, "Just for tonight. We have to keep moving."

I looked at Anna expectantly. She just exhaled, got up, and left. K.C. followed her, saying, "I'll tell everyone else."

So, the day was restful, sort of. Garrett and Will didn't approve of it, siding with Mark that we should keep going, but my friends and Mr. Maruken didn't put up any resistance.

"Stop touching your arm, Jamaica," Trace mumbled, eyes closed. We had scaled a tree to relax, but I was having a tough time leaving the cuts alone. They hurt, even if they weren't exposed. How was Trace able to leave his injuries alone?

I looked over and watched him as he took in the shaded light. I guess it wasn't unfathomable. All those years on his own had to have toughened him up. He probably never got to even be a kid.

"What happened all those years?" I comprehended saying it aloud when my boyfriend stirred, "What?"

"Nothing," I squeaked, but he rolled upright, shaking his head. "You said something, spit it out."

Hesitantly, I repeated, "What happened all those years? That you were running?"

He self-consciously glanced away. "It was stupid, forget I said anything-"

"Jamaica." I stopped. "I remember all seven years. Everything they did. Everything *I* did. I can tell you all of it, but…I like how you look at me now."

My brow creased. "I don't even like who I had to be just to stay afloat. If I told you, you wouldn't blush anymore. You wouldn't forgive me when I do something wrong or make you mad. You wouldn't…you wouldn't smile anymore."

Now it was my turn to sit up. "If you want me to, I'll go back through those memories. But you'll see the flaws that are better left alone. You're not going to see the me that's in front of you now."

"But what about Jamie? You told her the stories as she grew up."

"I told her pieces, just enough to give her a sense of adventure," he corrected, "Even my parents don't know what all I did. And as for me…I've left it behind. Sure, I've still got the skills, but I've been storing those memories away for a long time. Can I ask you to do the same?"

"What do you mean?"

"You know I've done things. I see you thinking about it when I slip up and make a comment. Take that knowledge, and just put it away. All that stuff shaped me, but it isn't me anymore. Unlocking it's just a mess."

"So we just hide the information?" I guessed. I got a half smile, and I think two signs. He cupped his right hand in front of his right shoulder, then moved it in a semicircle to the left one, keeping his palm facing his heart. Then he made the sign letter 'a'

90

(he'd managed to drill the alphabet into my head first and foremost) and pressed it thumb side against his mouth twice. "Our secret."

We heard twigs galore as someone rushed towards camp. Trace winced as he started to climb down, so I descended faster to compensate. The twigs slowed the louder they got, and I caught a flash of familiar blonde hair. "Ed?"

He stopped, completely panicked. I uneasily lowered onto the last branch, asking, "Are you- okay?"

"Please! Please, help me," he begged, "I can't- I can't-"

He began to hyperventilate, and I couldn't help but jump to the ground and try to calm him, not that it worked. It wasn't until Trace made it to us and talked him down that we could get anywhere. "Stop. Breathe. *Breathe.*"

It took a minute, but Ed did what he was told. Trace demanded, "What are you doing here? If you get caught-"

"Please! The Emperor- he-he-" The agent swallowed and ran his hands through his hair. Trace grabbed his shoulder and murmured, "Ed, you have to relax."

"He said he'd kill them, all of them-"

"Who?"

"My family," Ed choked, crumbling to his knees. He sat there a minute, just trying to get his lungs working properly before continuing, "If my partners and I don't bring someone back with us, he'll kill the people we love most. You have to understand, I don't have a lot of family left, and there's now a girl in danger because of me. I can't let anyone get hurt…"

He glanced past me and back, "…It wasn't part of the plan."

Life, Death, and Flight Plans

12

I looked behind me, but only saw Will teaching Mark about fire, Garrett watching them. I returned to the conversation as Trace interrogated, "What plan?"

"Look, I can't...no one knows what I'm doing at the OAD, and I need it to stay that way. If I'm found out as a traitor, I-"

"Ed," Trace spoke. Something about the way he talked seemed both authoritative and soothing. "I'll go with you."

Except for that. I protested, "Trace, that's insane-!"

"Why? They took me in the first place, it only makes sense-"

"He'll kill you! Look how much of you is wrapped up-"

"And who else is supposed to go? You?" I stopped mid word. "Jamaica, I can handle another night or two, it's okay. And I know you'll be right behind me. But you're the main target here. You need to stay where you're safest."

I wanted to argue that I wasn't some china doll that needed to stay on a shelf, but part of me knew he was right. He still reasoned, "I won't go right this minute. Ed, wait until later tonight, alright? It'll give us a chance to explain the situation to our team. Hey."

He knelt down in front of the agent and empathized, "I know what it's like to have family in danger. It's gonna be okay."

Trace helped him up and sent him off with a reassuring pat to the back. When the man was gone, I asked, "How did you do that?"

"Do what?"

"You just- you knew what to say." He stuffed his hands in his pockets, staring off in Ed's direction. "Another skill I picked up, I guess. C'mon, we should tell the others."

I can spread it almost all the way around.

Mugireti. I shouldn't have been surprised, he wasn't very far from us, but I still froze up.

Trace, you're absolutely sure?

Yes. Spread the message, Mugireti.

"Trace, you can't!" Jamie yelled indignantly. Everyone had gathered around the middle of the camp once the word spread.

"He's not goin'," Garrett huffed, but Trace challenged, "Yes, I am."

Garrett approached him, arms folded, but Trace didn't bother flinching. "Dan is gone. Cory is the only violent one, and Ed seems to more or less have a handle on him. And I've been captured plenty of times. I know how to stay out of trouble when I get to the facility."

The rider's irritation only seemed to worsen as Trace said this.

"James'll have you on a platter when he sees you roughed up," Garrett scolded, Trace shooting right back, "Let him."

Garrett loomed over him, questioning, "What is goin' on with you two and this agent? And since I can safely assume, why in the *hell* did he save me?"

"We don't know," I insisted, but my tongue suddenly got the spurt of courage to add, "Why are *you* so hung up on him?"

"Beg your pardon?" His jaw clenched, attention turning fully to me. And not only his. I had just become the center of focus. I guess I couldn't stop now. "You wanted to know who he was after he saved you. That's understandable. But now you're going berserk on us over Trace leaving with them, even though he's already done it before! If you really don't know who the man is, why does he suddenly matter so much?"

I quickly learned in that moment a very important lesson. Never put Garrett on the spot. His hands sparked, but not like Mark's. Not small wisps of fire. He had electricity running up and down the ridges of his bones. His head suddenly snapped over to Will, who had a very sympathetic expression. The elder's hands eased, tiny bolts steadily disappearing. Garrett finally grumbled, "Fine. Go with 'em. Get yourself killed."

And he strode back over to Mescheaf. But his frame was different now, like he could barely hold himself up. I gazed at Will in astonishment. "What did you say?"

Will sighed, "He has family, too. A wife and two boys. The younger one's only a year older than Trace, and if I've remembered right, the older would be about the same age of this agent by now."

"So, what? He thinks the agent is his son?" Mark skeptically concluded. Will explained, "His wife said the older ran off at eighteen. She doesn't know where he is. My guess is as good as yours, but Garrett's son has been on his mind ever since he got back last year. He's probably just connecting irrelevant strings out of desperation, and I really can't blame him."

Will and Mark continued to talk on their own, while Anna pulled Trace off to the side to talk privately. I noticed she looked perturbed, but didn't have a chance to think about it. Jamie marched up to me, saying, "You can't let him go."

"I can't stop him, Jamie. You know how he gets when his hero mode kicks in." She crossed her arms and puffed, "He turns into an idiot when that mode kicks in, you know that!"

"I know," I agreed. We both looked at him, finishing his conversation with Anna. She was still gleaming with discomfort, but opted to hide behind Pirsniketi than talk to anyone. Jamie shuffled away as Trace walked back over. "My sister's not happy with me leaving, is she?"

"She's not the only one," I hinted. He frowned, showing his understanding. I pushed forward, "What did Anna want?"

"She started asking about Cory," his eyebrows came together, "Like what he looked like, how tall he was. Wouldn't tell me why."

"Hm," I thought.

Trying to decode my men, Ms. Jamaica?

I bristled. It couldn't be.

Get out of my head. Get out!

Let's try something familiar, shall we?

Pain cracked through my head, and the 'M' on my left wrist lit up almost instantly. Trace cried out, "Jamaica!"

I toppled into him, losing my balance as I cradled my head.

Come now, surely that's not too much for a rider. You should be able to handle more than this.

The pain worsened, and I could only think to scream. My legs collapsed beneath me, and I caught pieces of voices from the team.

If this is torture, just give in. You cannot win.

No.

95

I struggled to keep pushing against the Emperor's presence. I couldn't let this happen. But if it did? No, he wasn't allowed to win. But if he did-?

Jamaica, relax! I can push him out, but you need to relax! If you keep trying to withstand this, you'll die!

I have to-

Jamaica, let me protect you!

The sentence struck me more than the pain. I was blinded by my wrist as I let go, hoping Mugireti would swoop in in time to take control of the situation. I heard the woman's scream even louder than ever as I passed out.

----0----

"Is she okay?!" Kaia worried. Jamaica was breathing shallow, and she wouldn't respond. Scarlet freaked out, "She's dead! Oh god, she's dead!"

"She's not dead!" Anna shouted, hands balling into fists, "She can't be-"

"Give her some room-" The moment Mark brushed his hand against Anna's shoulder, she shrieked, "Don't *touch* me, Frelck!"

He came within an inch away from her and commanded quietly, "Give her some room, or I swear-"

"Mark, she's breathing, I think Mugireti got ahold of it," K.C. reported. He was down on his knee in a second, immediately looking for a pulse. It was there, slower than usual, but there.

"Are either of you going to tell us what happened?" Trace prodded. Mark tried to ignore him as K.C. worked to stabilize their cousin's breathing. Trace shoved Mark in the shoulder, causing an immediate response of an elbow being pulled back for a punch. Trace barreled right into the words, "She was right in front of me,

96

and I couldn't do a thing. Don't expect me to just sit here without any idea of what just happened to her."

"It's Izoles," Mark shortly put, "He attacked her mind. It's not the first time either. Satisfied?"

Trace's jaw clenched as Mark lowered his arm and asked K.C., "How is she?"

"She'll be fine in a few minutes," she replied, "And you two better be civilized before she wakes up."

Mark watched his cousin intensely. She had to be okay. They needed her. She had to be okay. "We need to fly."

"Mark-"

"K.C., he's losing patience. If we keep waiting, he could attack her again, or someone else-"

"We're not bringing her injured and *unconscious* to the guy that wants to kill us!"

"We can't keep waiting!"

"Then meet in the middle," Trace forced. The two looked at him. "Mugireti says the forest's edge is probably half a day's flight from here. You'd be flying into the night, but he figures accounting for sleep, you can reach the OAD by sundown tomorrow. That gets you there quickly, and gives both Garrett and Jamaica recovery time. Sound like a plan?"

Mark hated to admit it, but it wasn't half bad. He reluctantly nodded with K.C. Trace informed everyone of the plan, and they immediately prepared to leave. Trace asked his father to ride Mugireti, as to keep Jamaica from slipping, because he had apparently set his heart on staying back to wait for that agent. Mark did have to wonder what the agent had done to get in favor of not only Trace, but Jamaica as well.

Mark, it is time to cool down.

He raised his hand without question, and Beuti rested her nose against it. Most of the anger washed away as he sensed her tranquility, and once his guard dropped, he realized he was only upset. Terrified, really. Izoles attacking Jamaica when they were this close was almost as bad as already being there. He caught himself as he started to lick his lips again.

She will be okay.

Mark wrapped his arms around Beuti's muzzle. "I know."

He lingered a second before climbing to the niche behind her neck. Anna waited for him, though they refused to say anything to each other.

He felt Beuti's muscles under him as she began to flap her wings and caught a glance at Trace as he waved everyone off, leaning against a tree and sitting down. He was gonna get himself killed.

----0----

An image of Cory, memories swirling around in his head. A burning house. A family inside. The Emperor offering assistance and accusing the riders.

An image of Fernando, piggybacking a little girl in pink overalls with her long dark hair in pigtails.

An image of Ed, a redheaded young lady in his arms, surrounded by obscured faces of who his family likely was. Except, there was some sort of break between him and his father.

"Is she okay?!"

"She's dead! Oh god, she's dead!"

"She's not dead! She can't be-"

"Hello? Guys?" I tried to call over the clamor. All I could see was white, like I was in an endless ivory room.

"She was right in front of me, and I couldn't do a thing. Don't expect me to just sit here without any idea of what just happened to her."

"Trace?" I shouted, my voice echoing. No reply, and now the voices were silent. I murmured, "What's going on?"

"Jamaica." Shock hit me as I spun around. That was a voice I never thought I'd hear. "M-Mom?"

"Hi, muffin." I couldn't help running to hug her. For a split second, I thought it would be like the movies, where it would just be an illusion, and I would run through her. But I crashed into her fully solid form, squeezing her as tight as I could so nothing could take her away. I was sobbing, I knew that much. But I only registered her arms coming around me as she sadly delighted, "Oh, you've grown right under my nose, haven't you?"

"You're alive," I croaked. She didn't answer. I pulled back to see her biting her lip. "Jamaica. You're in your subconscious. I'm fabricated from your memory and imagination."

Normally, I would have asked what fabricated meant. But my heart sunk as I gathered the context clues. "Then…then you really- *are* dead?"

"Well, I don't know," She said with curiosity, looking around at the white space, "Like I said, I'm created up here."

She tapped the side of my head. She shrugged, "Who's to say I'm dead? Who's to say I'm not?"

Someone cleared their throat behind her. Courtney? My past life? "Oh, it looks like you'll be waking up soon. I have to go now."

"Wait, Mom-"

"I'm always in your head, muffin. You know how to find me." Courtney winked at me as she led Mom away, and they both faded into nothing. "Mom!"

"Oh, such a pity." I whipped around to see Izoles standing behind me. I gulped, "You're not real."

"Maybe not," he confessed, "But I'm certainly real enough to scare *you*."

His voice thundered, making the air shake. I stuttered, "St-Stop it!"

"You cannot stop me." I blinked, and everything was dark. I was running, faster and faster, but not fast enough. I fell to the ground, and a gash opened up across my back. I lay in a pool of blood, scornful laughter filling my ears.

And then the scene changed. No more blood, no gash. But it was the Emperor's throne room. On my left, my mother and a little boy. On my right, Mark and K.C. In front of me, Trace. My cousins and boyfriend all looked a few years older, and all five people had weapons at their throats. I felt like I was standing in a photograph. No one was moving, but each looked like they were in the middle of an action.

"Who will it be?" The Emperor's voice boomed, "Your team, who you swore deepest bonds to? Maybe your long-lost piece of family? Or possibly the love of your life?"

I just stared. What was I supposed to do? Mark and K.C. were so much more than just cousins. I would give anything to save them. But then there was my Mom, and that random little boy. And Trace. I didn't know if I would call him 'the love of my life,' but he was still just as important to me as the others.

The- vision, I guess?- started to dissolve, and I pleaded, "No! Wait!"

If I tried to grab at any part of it, my hand came back with a mound of particles that spilled away like sand. And then I was left in grey. The word 'choose' was unheard and unseen, but I felt its crushing weight on top of me, pushing me down until I fell on my back. Pressing until I thought I would be flattened-

Wind. I could feel it fluttering my hair, causing goosebumps on my skin. I felt my back slowly bend until I could tell I was draped over something. Movement, steady and strong. Even in my clouded mind, I recognized it almost immediately as the beats of dragon wings. My nerves began to wake up, and I could feel the unevenness of scales beneath me. Pain in my left arm. The two cuts, that's right.

I opened my eyes, but my sight took its time adjusting. I saw a blonde figure sitting tall, though, and my first reaction was, "Trace?"

That's when my eyes became useful again, allowing me to see that it was actually his father Jack. He had late afternoon sun shining on him, making him resemble his son even more than usual.

Mugireti.

Jamaica! Oh, thank goodness!

Where's Trace? Why are we flying?

Well- after you passed out there was a bit of bickering between Mark, K.C., and Trace, that basically ended with us flying to the forest edge and him staying behind to wait for your agent.

A pang of sadness anchored itself in my gut.

They'll make it to the OAD in the morning if they fly through the night. With us stopping for rest, we should be there by late afternoon tomorrow.

How long have we been flying?

Ten minutes, fifteen maybe. Why?

Distance check. Trace?

No answer.

Trace!

Jamaica? Thank god.

You stayed behind?

I had prior engagements.

I heard the humor he tried to put into it. He was trying to make it sound less serious than it was.

Be careful.

I felt the slight hesitation in his thoughts.

I will.

I raised my hand to tap Mr. Maruken's thigh. He jumped a little, but didn't resist when I used him as a human jungle gym to get myself sitting properly on Mugireti. I watched the sky over the next few hours as it faded from blue, to red, to black. Maybe it was just paranoia, but what if something happened to Trace? It wasn't an unreasonable concern, all things considered.

Jamaica.

Hm?

We're landing in a minute. Just stay awake a little longer, alright?

Okay.

I hadn't realized how tired I was until Mugireti told me stay awake. I saw the forest fall back to reveal a sea of meadow grass, turned a silvery lavender by the moonlight. Pretty.

I held Mugireti's neck tighter as he landed, shaking the ground with the other dragons. I slid off and looked over just in time to see Garrett take a hard fall. That gave me a shot of adrenaline, and I ran over. The oldest rider was spitting curses as he roughly pushed himself up, Mescheaf trying to help him. "Garrett!"

"I'm fine," he grunted, getting to his feet, "Just a case a' damn paresthesia."

"Para- what?" I repeated as Jamie slipped down the gold dragon's back. Mescheaf lay down, allowing her rider to ease down next to her. I noted that all his weight was on his left leg. He clarified, "Paresthesia. My leg fell asleep. And since I wasn't payin' attention, it just about cost my ankle."

He explained it two or three more times as the rest of the group came running, while I trudged back over to Mugireti.

Is he alright?

Yeah, nothing too bad, from what it sounds like.

I plopped down against his stomach, yawning.

Forgive me if I'm prying, but while you were out of it, I noticed a lot of brain activity going on.

I told him everything. About my mom, about the Emperor, about- the vision. As I said it all, I tried to make sense of it. Were we really still going to be in this mess years from now? Would I really have to choose who to save?

Get some rest. You'll need all your strength tomorrow.

Just as I went to lay down, a helicopter zoomed overhead, and I got a sudden twinge of pain on the right side of my ribcage. "Mugireti, something's wrong."

They've been flying behind us the whole time, Jamaica.

But Trace-

I know you're worried about him, but he said it himself. He can handle them.

That didn't explain the sudden bit of pain, but I was too tired to argue. I curled into him and watched his wing come down with my eyelids.

Insight

13

It was a relief to hear Jamaica's voice, to know she was alright. And not a moment too soon, as Trace caught Ed approaching. The boy got up without a word to follow the agent back. As they walked in silence, Trace glanced over, and an idea popped into his head.

So, you're like me.

Ed's jaw clenched.

Yes.

Trace grinned. It was a reluctant answer, but one nonetheless.

Did it give you a headache when the animal voices first showed up?

Not really. But my abilities have only been around about a year and a half. They could still be settling in. Although…

Ed chuckled a little out loud.

I can't say I expected the tail.

Trace's brow knit.

A tail?

Yeah, it freaked me out. I hate to say, but Dan had to teach me to control it.

Control the- tail?

What the hell was he talking about? Ed looked over, and comprehension washed over him. "You've never changed before, have you?"

"Changed?" A small smile tugged at the corner of the young man's mouth. "I'll tell you what. If we both make it out of this trip alive, I'll teach you what I know. And maybe you can tell me about those headaches. I might need to prepare-"

Trace knew he should've been alert. Seven years running should've drilled that into his head. But he'd started to feel at ease, knowing Ed had the same ability, and could possibly teach him more. Now he was hunched over on his knees, desperately covering as much of the cut in his side with his hands as he could. He watched as Ed shoved Cory to the ground, snarling, "What are you thinking?! Fernando, get the medical kit!"

Fernando ran to the copter to get it. Trace could feel his own blood streaming past his fingers, and pain raking up and down his torso. Ed was still letting loose his fury, "-thought you were better than that! Better than Dan! I told you, we're not *killers*!"

"Ed! I got it!" Fernando called, rushing back over. Ed grabbed it from him and quickly shuffled through the supplies, commanding, "Fernando, hold him down!"

"Which one?!" One deadly look, and he completely understood. The brown skinned agent laid Trace on his side, and then backwards against his thigh. But Trace wasn't about to let him pry his hands away. Ed came into view, demanding, "Trace you have to trust me-"

"Is that wire?!" Fernando gasped, Ed retorting, "Shut up, it's all we've got! Trace, please, trust me!"

105

Trace didn't really see much of another option. Fernando brought the boy's arms over his head and held them there as a needle suddenly pierced Trace's skin, just over his hip. Trace squirmed and screamed, but Ed was unyielding, quickly sewing the cut as best he could. The stitches weren't uniform, but they held the cut closed enough that Fernando was ordered to grab a towel, which Ed was then strapping to Trace's side. "We have to get him to Matt. I'll keep an eye on him so he doesn't bleed out in the night, but Matt's the only one who can give him proper stitches."

"I'll get the helicopter ready." Fernando sprinted back towards the cockpit as Ed hefted Trace into his arms. Trace soon lay across two helicopter seats, Ed buckling him in, then disappearing for a minute. He came back, hauling Cory over and hissing, "Count yourself lucky that we're not leaving you behind."

Cory strapped himself in next to Fernando as Ed did so in the seat under Trace's legs, and the copter was airborne. Ed instructed, "Trace, do not fall asleep. I will slap you, punch you even, if I have to. You cannot fall asleep, understand? You fall asleep, you could be done for."

Trace nodded weakly. He found it hard to believe that he would fall asleep under this much pain.

Hours went by, and the only light to be seen was the illumination of the control board. How Trace hadn't gone into shock was beyond him. Or maybe he was, and just didn't realize it.

"Ed!" Fernando yelled over his shoulder, "We've hit the halfway point! Just passed over the riders!"

Jamaica. Trace had promised her he'd be careful. Technically, the predicament wasn't his fault, but that didn't stop him from mentally cursing.

Well, at least you're still conscious.
How much longer?

Just a few more hours, hang in there. And try not to scream.

Try not to-?

Ed peeled the towel off, and Trace couldn't restrain the howl that escaped him. The agent was quick to press a fresh one over top of the cut, using new medical tape to keep it in place.

Had to be replaced. I've got to do what I can to keep you from getting infected.

I'm going to die, aren't I?

Trace had meant it as a grab for reassurance. So when Ed paused, he could've sworn his heart stopped.

I hope not.

The flight dragged out longer after that. Trace remembered getting slapped once, maybe twice, as exhaustion started to set in. And why shouldn't it have? The sky was grey from the crack of dawn. Ed had gotten him to stay up all night.

The agent encouraged, "You're doing great, Trace, just hold out a little longer."

He was trying, hoping that once the sky was blue again, the light would be enough to keep him awake.

Trace fought to keep his eyelids open as the helicopter slowed. The agony of his side couldn't overcome his want for sleep. He watched as Ed fought off the horde of hands that reached in to grab at him. He lay limp as Ed picked him up again. He didn't pay attention to where Ed took him, only noticing the brainwashing machine when they were right next to it. With the little strength he had, Trace shied away from it, Ed coaxing, "It's alright, we're not going there."

He walked through another door at the back of the room, and Trace heard, "Ay Dios mio."

The next thing Trace registered was that he was on a cot with a boy about his age frantically searching over his side. "You

107

used fiber to cover the wound, you didn't disinfect, this mess of wire is barely holding him closed- were you *trying* to kill him-?!"

"I did what I could with what I had!"

"Westyn," came a familiar Spanish accent, "Regardless of his mistakes, he very well may have saved the boy's life. Por favor, let us take it from here."

"O-Of course," Ed complied, "Just take care of him, okay?"

Ed left, and Trace forced himself to look around. The Spanish man. Trace remembered he had called him the Operator, because he had controlled the machine in the other room. So he was a medic as well, it seemed. The boy next to him was checking vitals, from his pulse to his temperature. Trace thought he saw green eyes behind the shaggy dark hair, but didn't get to dwell on it, letting out a cry as the other boy tried to remove the towel. The Operator commanded, "Gentle, Westyn."

"The stitching is terrible, it's amazing he didn't bleed out-"

"Stop criticizing and fix it, or he absolutely will!" The boy, Westyn, immediately grabbed a bottle, and carefully pulled off the towel. "Okay, man, just- hold still, this is gonna sting."

Trace's side burned as Westyn applied what was likely a disinfectant. The pain became nauseating, to the point Trace was sure he'd pass out.

Trace.

"Jamaica," he slurred. He had to stay awake. He couldn't die, couldn't leave her. Westyn froze when Trace spoke, and whispered in awe, "What did you just say?"

Trace!

I'm here.

Are you okay?

Well…it's debatable.

Trace this isn't funny, what happened?

I'm-I'm fine. Getting my injuries cleaned by a professional. The-The disinfectant just burns.

108

There was a pause. He felt her worry, and tried to send soothing thoughts over.

We're heading out. We should be there by late afternoon.

He moaned in frustration. He wanted to be there in the throne room with her, to protect her. Wasn't that what a boyfriend was supposed to do? His back arched as Westyn touched up the top of the cut. "Take it easy, I'm trying to be fast."

Trace?!

He cut the connection. Jamaica would feel that pain, she would know something was wrong. "Matt, I need help with this."

The man came over as Westyn explained, "The wire has to be cut so actual stitches can go in, but I'll have to pinch the ends so the rest of it doesn't unravel. I can't stitch with one hand, though."

"I'll stitch, you focus on keeping the wire taut." Trace began to nod off, but Westyn patted his cheek, "Don't pass out. Not until Matt says it's okay."

Matt's hands worked quickly to stitch the wound, but Trace started to lose ground. He wanted nothing more than to shut his eyes- pop! A solid palm to the cheek. "C'mon, stay awake."

"Shut- up," Trace groaned. If he'd had the strength, he would've shoved the boy, but god, he couldn't. His body was shutting down, wanting to recharge. So, there was another slap. "Stop."

"If I stop, you'll pass out, and if you pass out, you die. Matt, can we shoot adrenaline in him or something?"

"Just keep him conscious a little longer." Trace lost count of how many times Westyn had to snap him back, or even how much time passed before Matt was on the other end of the cut. He finished off the last stitch, and then murmured, "Alright. You can sleep now."

Just before he went under, Trace heard, "Did you hear the name he said? He knows Jamaica-"

"Do not meddle, Westyn. Just get me a pack of o-negative for transfusion…"

A Father's Perspective

14

"Is everyone ready?" I asked reluctantly. K.C. nodded, a solemn expression on her face.

Let's go over the instructions again.

Mugireti-

We land once we get to the rocks and climb from that point on. And we'll have to expect capture-

Mugireti, I know the plan. We've already run through it three times this morning.

We have to make sure the details are sorted out.

I didn't reply as I watched everyone review the plan as well.

If the mission weren't so important, I wouldn't have flown you. You know that.

I know. I still think I should check in on him. I felt something last night, I know something happened.

I don't see what you expect to find, but be my guest.

Trace.

Nothing. It could've been distance, but I tried again anyway.

Trace!

I'm here.

He absolutely was, and I could feel tremendous pain.

Are you okay?

Well...it's debatable.

I could've sworn I actually heard a chuckle in his voice. Something definitely wasn't right if he was joking about his well-being.

Trace, this isn't funny, what happened?

I'm-I'm fine. Getting my injuries cleaned by a professional. The-The disinfectant just burns.

I knew he was lying, but I didn't refuse the calmness he sent over the connection.

We're heading out. We should be there by late afternoon.

I hadn't expected what happened next. A sudden flash of pain raked up my side, causing me to double over and fall to my knees.

Trace?!

The line broke off sharply, the pain disappearing. "Jamaica!"

Mark knelt down in front of me, inquiring, "Hey, what is it? What happened?"

"It's Trace," I breathed, "I think he's been hurt."

"He has cuts covering his chest, of course he's-"

"No, something new, Mark. Something on his side." He paused before muttering, "Then I guess we better get moving."

Everyone took to the dragons, and we were in the air in under a minute. Thoughts zoomed back and forth through my mind in a flurry.

Jamaica, you need to calm down-

I can't calm down, Mark! He's been hurt! And a cut like that could kill him!

We're talking about Trace here. I may not be fond of him, but I won't say he isn't resilient.

Resilient or not, he could lose a lot of blood. We need to get to the facility-

Jamaica, the dragons are flying as fast they can. Trust me, we'll get there.

I knew that sound in his voice. He hated every beat of Beuti's wings right now. And if Bruno weren't a captive too, he probably wouldn't have come.

In just a few hours, my feet hit gravel and the group started to climb the boulders ahead.

"Can't we fly all the way?" Scarlet complained. I replied, "Sure. And we'll get pulled to the ground and dragged across the facility to meet up with the Emperor."

No one argued after that. The hike was long and uncomfortably silent, and when we reached the gates, I turned to my three friends. "There's still time to turn back. If any of you want to, we can send you home on one of the dragons-"

"We've come too far, Jamaica," Anna intervened, "We're not going to leave you now."

"The Emperor's gonna get what he deserves," Scarlet agreed. Kaia adjusted the quiver strap on her shoulder and added, "We didn't sign up to run."

I pursed my lips. I couldn't ask for better friends. So why had I pulled them into this? "Then be prepared."

"Will, would ya like to do the honors?" Garrett offered. Both had an excited grin that seemed misplaced, compared to the trip. Will cracked his knuckles and sent a hurricane worthy gust into the front gates, dozens of bodies flying from where they had hidden against the inside walls. But no sooner did the wind die, more guards swarmed out. I fought down the instinct to resist, feeling hands roughly grab my arms and steal my dagger away. Like the others, I was shoved through a jeering crowd of faces, only hearing the groan of oak doors before landing on my knees. When the extra men and women cleared out, I realized that I was the only one not on my feet.

"I see you've brought friends, Ms. Jamaica." There was that jolt of fear. I had thought for a split second I might not get it. The Emperor strode up to me, but I wouldn't look up. Those cat green eyes would trap me in my own fear, I knew it.

"Get away from her!" I heard Anna shout. No, Anna don't call attention to yourself-

"Why, Anna Baker. I haven't seen your sweet little face in years." The words reeled me back into reality, giving me the courage to glance over at my best friend. Short hairs hung loose on the sides of her face, but she was in no way afraid. She stood tall and proud, and though shock and anger mixed in her eyes, they only created something more dangerous.

"I've never *met* you," she growled, "but you hurt my best friend, and you won't get away with it!"

"Dear Anna," he began to approach her, "What's the last thing you remember of him, hm? Your brother?"

The atom bomb button. The mention that would make her lose it. In seconds, she was screaming at the top of her lungs, wildly struggling to the point the guard had to lift her off the ground by her waist to carry her out of the room because she was physically clawing at the Emperor.

She may be a hard head, but that was uncalled for.

I watched Mark's fist curl behind him. However, the Emperor was more interested in the older riders. Garrett wore an expression of age old loathing, but Will...Will looked like he was about to be punished. "Well, if it isn't my favorite prisoners. You've returned once more, it seems."

"Keep your sophistication, James, ya know we don't buy it," Garrett chided. The Emperor chuckled, "You don't need to. I think we all know that I've kept my eyes on both of you, as always. How are your wife and *son*?"

Garrett ground his jaw, but said nothing, so Izoles continued, "And you, William, are you still searching?"

Searching-? The room lit up as fire streamed from Will's mouth. When it finally died down, Will was hunched over, and I could've sworn I saw a spark of electricity dance up his thigh. His teeth gritted, he threatened, "I'll kill you."

"My boy, you've tried." With a wave of Izoles' hand, Will was hauled from the room, and Garrett soon after when he called the Emperor a coward, with a few colorful words thrown in for enhancement. Mark tried to roll his shoulders back, but the guard punched him in the spine. I flinched and closed my eyes. "Ah, Mr. Frelck."

"Bastard," he said under his breath. Another hit, and he went down on one knee, some of the air knocked out of his lungs. "One would think after learning about your father, you would be keener to show me the due respect."

"What respect do you deserve?" Mark hissed, "You're a murderer."

"And a merciless one at that," the Emperor warned, laying a hand on the hilt of his sword, "Tell me, do you remember how bright the explosion was? Or how loud your mother screamed? Because I recall every detail as if it were yesterday. And I enjoy reliving every second-"

"You're insane," Mark bared his teeth, "You killed an innocent man and it *amuses* you!"

"I have no qualms with doing it again-"

"No!" K.C. blurted, shifting toward Mark. She immediately rocked back on her heels when Izoles gazed at her, but he was fixated, purring, "Now you speak in my presence? Your bravery is dwindling, Katherine."

He had her cornered, in a sense. She couldn't look away, but anyone could've seen how much she wanted to. Her lip trembled slightly, and he finally continued, "It seems your courage has shrunk to a single word. Have you nothing more to say?"

He was inches away from her, and I could see her leaning back- "Touch her and I will *maim* you."

"With what, dear boy?" The Emperor replied to Mark, not breaking eye contact with our redheaded cousin, "Your anger only makes you reckless. You would more likely bring harm to those close to you, such as your father."

Mark snapped and lunged, and the Emperor was pleased, having my cousins removed. Kaia flinched the moment he looked over, so he merely waved her away as well. He crossed in front of me, though, when he saw Scarlet. He didn't bother with Mr. Maruken or Jamie either, even when they demanded to know where Trace was. Izoles just sent them out like the others. He only saw Scarlet, glaring vehemently back at him. His emotions, on the other hand didn't make sense. "My little girl. After all these years, you've found your way back to me."

"I'm not your 'little girl,'" she spat, looking him over, "And I'd certainly never want to be."

"Come now, Ida never told you? You're no Jones, Scarletine." She sucked in a breath, and I couldn't help mumbling, "Scarletine?"

"You-You know-? How do you know my name?! No one is supposed to know my name!" she protested. He proceeded, "No one except your parents."

"Burt Jones is my father."

"Oh, how Ida must have deceived you. Burt Jones is your stepfather. He adopted you when you were but a few months old. But I know Ida's face anywhere, even in our children-"

"You're not my father!" she denied, but he kept pushing, "Then tell me how I would know about the two birthmarks on your back, or that your mother's favorite flower is a black rose? Or even, that you have black hair and Asian features, baring little resemblance to Ida and none at all to Burt?"

"Stop it!" I suddenly yelled, "All you do is manipulate, you don't expect her to actually believe you-?"

"Jamaica," Scarlet tried in a small voice. Her voice had never been so tiny and soft before. I said certain things I shouldn't have, I'll admit to it. But as Izoles walked back towards me, my stomach dropped. I was going to regret every word. "I see your arm is injured. But clearly, you still have the moxie to speak against me under pressure."

A gesture of his hand, and my left arm was forced out, held parallel to the ground. I couldn't move, and my breath came shallower and shorter as he unsheathed his sword.

I'm gonna lose my arm, he's gonna cut it off-

There was a slice alright, but it dragged out as long as the Emperor could go. He didn't amputate anything, but steadily traced down my arm, splitting my skin. I screamed and tried to pull away, but he laughed, "You'll only lengthen the cut by knocking me off course, Ms. Jamaica."

Blood was already spilling onto the floor by the time he was done. So much blood. "Take her to Matt. Maybe once she survives this, she will learn her place."

I felt myself going into shock, and tried to fight it. I'd survived this before, I could do it again. But I'd also been out cold for several days…

The guard was quick, scooping me up and taking me across the grounds in moments. I didn't see where we were going, only felt my back hit a bed. My vision began to blur and darken, but I remember hearing, "Dios mio."

Someone began working on my arm, and put a light weight on my chest, but I blacked out a second later, hearing that scream loud enough to send my ears ringing.

----0----

I opened my eyes drowsily and looked around. I had to be in some sort of hospital room. The walls were a light mint and there were several cabinets not far away on the opposite wall. It looked a lot like the room in the workshop. But how did I get here? What *day* was it-?!

Pain came to life in my left arm, and I caught sight of the wrap. Ace bandages, actual medical Ace bandages. As I moved, I realized it was across my chest and back too. When I brushed my fingers down my arm, there was a continuous line of bumps, stitches, I assumed. Who had done this-?

A soft groan emanated next to me. I looked over and sighed in a little relief. Things always felt a little safer with a familiar face around, and right now, it was Trace's neutral expression as he slept. His shirt had been stitched up, and a little bit of Ace bandage peeked out from his sleeve. There was even an empty blood bag hanging next to him. Someone had tended to his injuries too.

My eyes drifted back to his face, calm and unperturbed. It wasn't something I saw very often. He always had something on his mind, and it always showed. And just like that, the serenity ended. His eyelids drifted back, his brow inched together in confusion, and then his face screwed tight in pain. He held his right side, gasping, and it only seemed to worsen if he tried to sit up. "Trace."

He glanced over at his name, replying, "Jamaica?"

He let out a small growl, throwing his head backward into his pillow. As if on cue, a darker, older man rushed in. Seeing Trace's squirming, he quickly went to the cabinets. In seconds, he

118

was at Trace's side with a syringe, and Trace immediately shifted away from him. "It is a pain reliever, calm down."

He took Trace's arm and injected something into his bloodstream. The result was quick. Trace began to relax, even though his jaw stayed clenched. "Better?"

The man reached over and removed the needle taped into Trace's hand, disconnecting him from the empty blood packet. When he turned around, his eyes skipped across me, and his shoulders became tense. He went back to the cabinets, filling a different syringe with a lesser dose of the pain reliever. When he approached me, he clarified, "For your arm."

The faded accent to his voice tugged at my brain, but I dismissed it. I didn't move as he gave me the shot, save for a small fidget when the needle broke skin. The numbing came along in seconds. The man went back to clean the syringes, commenting, "It is amazing what our bodies can recover from, but that does not justify such wounds to be made. Now which one of you will be the first to tell me what happened?"

I traded looks with my boyfriend, and he blurted, "Agent that turned aggressive."

"Cory did that?" I breathed. Which other agent could he have been talking about? He nodded. The man turned to me, hesitantly pressing, "And you?"

Trace sat up a little, wincing as he tried to see. I sat up too, cradling my injured arm. His eyes lit up with horror and anger. I mumbled, "The Emperor."

"He's gonna pay," Trace grunted, grabbing the edge of the bed. His side reminded him that he was wounded, and the ends of his pillow puffed up as he fell back into it. The man ran his fingers through his hair and began to pace. A slight memory of Izoles' words came back to me. "Are you Matt?"

"What?" he responded, a look of terror washing over him briefly. I shrugged my good shoulder, "He told the guard to take me to 'Matt.' Is that you?"

"You would hate me if you knew who I was," he dodged. I reasoned, "You saved both our lives. It would be kind of unfair to hate you."

When he didn't answer, Trace did, "He had an assistant calling him Matt. Westyn, right?"

"You two need your rest," he insisted, licking the side of his lips, "and if you break any of your stitches, I'll have you restrained."

"Wait!" I inhaled, staring at him. I thought his face looked familiar, but I'd ignored the thought. Until he licked his lips. I chanced, "Mr. Frelck?"

His fear increased, and he stiffened completely. "Jamaica, let me explain-"

"You're alive," I choked on my shock, "You're alive and you work for *him*?"

"It was hardly my choice-"

"How could you?! You should be protecting your son! He thinks you're dead!" I shouted, anger rushing to my brain faster than I could think, "You should be helping Mark-!"

"I am helping him!" His voice rose, full and loud. I shrunk back at the sound. Trace watched Matt warily as he walked over to me, cautiously sitting at the foot of my bed. The man hunched over as he divulged, "The Emperor knew about you kids from the moment Mark was born. When he took your mother, the rest of the parents decided it would be for the best that you all were kept secret. Your father went so far as to keep your cousins out of your knowledge, and you out of theirs."

"That doesn't explain anything," I huffed. He continued, "When Mark was seven, I created a device that could shock people-"

"You made those things-?!" Trace spat, agitating his side again. Matt pleaded, "It was meant to be harmless, a means of waking up an exhausted brain during long hours. A small vibration that would keep nerves sending signals to the brain at the user's will. But my invention allowed the Emperor to make his next move. He came to my lab one night when I was expecting Mark and his mother, and forced a deal on me."

"What deal?" I pushed, some of the rage starting to ebb. "If I faked my death, came to work for him, and weaponized my creation, Mark could live like a normal child, at least until he found his dragon."

"And if you didn't?" Trace inquired, making Matt swallow, "He had an armed bomb on my desk ticking down. If I refused, he would lock me in my office to be blown to smithereens with the rest of the building. Then, he would kill Mark and his mother when they arrived."

I thought about the night from Mark's perspective. To see all of that, and never even know… "Understand, if I had seen a way out, I would have taken it. Even as his men led me out, the explosion threw us to the ground at the outside door. I had not known my son and wife were already present. I ran into him, Jamaica. He was trying to go in after me. I knew of his powers, but I knocked him over and got to the shadows as fast as I could."

"Why didn't you just show him you were alright?" I insisted. He shook his head, "I feared the Emperor would go back on the deal. Even my son bumping into me, or Janice pulling him back so fast- I thought he would surely consider the deal null and void. But he held to his word, even stopping one of the guards from taking Mark from Janice."

"I can be a man of my word." All eyes darted to the doorway as Izoles himself entered. Trace struggled up onto his elbows, and the usual energy began to buzz in my muscles. But instead of feeling scared, I suddenly felt very determined. I climbed out of the bed, legs wobbling and unable to keep my balance. Matt got to his feet, ordering, "Jamaica, you've lost blood, please-"

"No," I denied, attention zeroed in on my enemy, "You're a dirty player, and an absolute coward-"

"And you are seriously injured. If I were you, I wouldn't be so quick to insult the one who caused your wound. It's really not your brightest idea, my little rider-"

"I'm not your 'little rider,'" I spat, noticing Trace's fists curled out of the corner of my eye. Izoles, unfazed, mused, "I see you've met your uncle."

"You've got nothing over him," I dared, but he just smirked, "It seems you still haven't learned."

I flinched when he tried to hit me, but opened one eye when it never came. Matt had caught the Emperor's wrist. "Unhand me, Mr. Frelck."

"Mark found his dragon, releasing me of your deal. For six years, I have remained under your command of my own accord. I will act against you if it means protecting my family from unnecessary harm." The Emperor pulled his hand back, and Matt commanded, "Jamaica. Get back in that bed."

I unsteadily made it back to the bed as Izoles sneered, "You forget, your son is in the facility as we speak. All it would take is my word, and he would be dead."

"What can you do?" I scoffed, "He's immune to anything with heat or light-"

"Jamaica, *be quiet*." My sentence stopped there with the cold glare that Matt gave me. He turned back to Izoles. "It may be your facility, but this is my work space. That being said, I cannot do my job with such an atmosphere, and will politely ask only once that you leave."

The Emperor made a mocking sound with his heartless smile before leaving without another word. Matt pointed at Trace and snapped, "Lay down and do not sit up again unless I tell you to."

Trace hesitantly did as he was told. Matt's attention then turned to me, "And you. Stay in that bed. You may have more mobility than him, but you still need rest before you start moving around."

He walked back to the cabinets, wagging his finger, "If I catch either of you disobeying me-"

"You'll have us restrained, we know," Trace exasperatedly sighed. When Matt and I just stared at him, he puffed, "We hear that a lot, actually."

"Fabuloso," Matt grumbled, "If you'll excuse me, I have a special patient to check on."

He hooked a stethoscope around his neck and packed a small kit together before walking out the door. "So, he doesn't want us moving, but then he leaves us unattended?"

"Maybe he's sending Westyn in," Trace suggested. I asked, "Who's Westyn?"

"I don't know. I mean, I half met him, but I can't imagine what he's doing here. He's only about our age."

Jamaica, can you hear me?

Mark?

Where are you?! I've been trying to get ahold of you for at least an hour!

Sorry, I...

"Jamaica?" Trace gave me an inquisitive look.

I was asleep, I guess. Or maybe I passed out.

Passed out? What happened?

"Jamaica, what is it?" Trace insisted. I answered, "Mark's about to panic, if he isn't already."

"Mark? How are you-?"

Jamaica!

"Shut up, I can't talk to two people at once," I hushed my boyfriend, maybe a bit rudely.

Scarlet was in the room with me, she didn't tell you?

She's been a statue since they brought her into the cells. Whatever he did after K.C. and I were taken out shell-shocked her.

I paused, biting the inside of my cheek, the new information about Scarlet bubbling up in my head. And I decided it wasn't best to tell Mark that.

Mark, my right and left arms just became twins.

What?

My right arm is scarred. And now my left arm will look just like it.

The pause in the conversation churned my stomach. His emotions bombarded my head, anger swelling in my skull and fear freezing up my muscles.

Where are you?

Rebirth

15

"So, you managed to unlock your connection with Mark?" Trace questioned, interested in the fact that I'd been able to mentally communicate with my cousin. I could see the small pang of jealousy in his eyes, but he wouldn't let it show anywhere else. "I think by deciding to tell me what happened that night, he brought us to a deep enough level of trust that we made a full connection."

"Maybe," he countered, "but what about K.C.? Do you not have enough trust between you two?"

"The needed connection could be different between us," I suggested, but Trace disagreed, "Trust is a stressed thing in all your lessons with Jeff. I would think it's a common bond to be earned."

"Dude, who are you talking to-?" A boy with shaggy dark hair walked in, stilling when he laid eyes on me. He just stared at me in shock, clearly not expecting me to be here. After a long, very awkward silence, Trace cautiously introduced, "So…this is Westyn. I think."

At his name, Westyn blinked and appeared to remember what he had come here for. Without a word, he went to the cabinets and grabbed a white bottle and cotton pads. Walking over to Trace, he explained, "I need to clean your chest to be sure you don't get infected."

The boy met no resistance to rolling up Trace's shirt and removing the bandages. My boyfriend bit back a groan as a dampened pad touched his chest. "Yeah, sorry, it's gonna sting."

"Westyn," I mulled the name over. I'd never heard it before. The owner of it froze a second before continuing on. Trace asked, "What's gotten into you?"

"Nothing," Westyn sharply answered, focusing on his task. I pressed, "Who are you? Why are you here when you're only our age? If Izoles threatened you, we can protect you-"

"You *can't*," he aggressively hissed, "There are many things riders can do. That's not one of them. You can't protect me from him."

"Why not?" He paused, face screwed into a sort of agonized sadness. His tone didn't waver though as he replied, "Because if he knows I'm helping you, then god have mercy. His wrath extends past what you're able to shield. Trust me."

A low *BOOM* made some of the tools in the cabinets rattle. Westyn stopped his work with a confused, "What the…?"

He shuffled out of the room, leaving Trace and me to glance at each other in equal bafflement. It wasn't long before Westyn ran back in, panting, "What's your cousin's name again?"

Jamaica, I'm coming to get you, where are you?

Building across the facility from the throne room. Mark-

"Which one?" Trace pushed, but I readily answered, "Mark, Matt's son."

126

"Matt's *son*-?" Said son tackled him with a war cry, a blazing fist already in place for a blow-

"Mark, stop! Stop!" A quick gust blew Mark's hand out like a candle, allowing Westyn to scramble out from under him. My cousin stood up, sparks lighting his palms. "Jamaica, you okay?"

"Sort of- Mark, he's not gonna hurt us-"

"We're getting out of here-"

"We can't-"

"J, don't be stubborn-"

"We can't leave Trace!" Mark glanced over at my boyfriend and after a clear moment of conflict, extinguished his hands and barked, "Patch him up!"

"He needs time to rest!" Westyn protested. Mark yelled over him, "He doesn't have time! Now fix him, or I swear, I'll-!"

"You're in my way!" The tension built between the two until Mark sidestepped, leaning against my cot. Westyn cautiously rose, edging past the hothead to examine Trace's side. "We're in a hurry-"

"Not until I say so," Westyn snapped, courage seeping into him. Mark growled, "If Izoles finds us-"

"If you let me do my job, he won't!" Westyn retorted, a small, sharp medical tool in hand pointed at Mark. Matt's assistant set the tool down and continued to look at Trace. I caught Mark lick his lips several times as he glanced at the door.

How's your arm?

Mark folded his arms, trying to ease his fidgeting.

It's...It's fine. Westyn- gave me a pain reliever.

You trusted a kid our age to give you medicine?

He knows more about medicine than we do.

How do you know that-?

Am I dead?

J-

Am I dead?

He looked down at me, uncertainty resting into annoyance. *You trust him?*

Truthfully, I didn't. I trusted the man who had actually given the dose. But something in my gut told me this would be just about the worst time to tell Mark that.

He helped keep Trace alive.

"He can't leave," Westyn concluded. Mark and I adlibbed, "What?"

"What do you mean I can't leave?" Trace huffed, voice cracking. Westyn insisted, "You barely have the strength to lean on your elbows, let alone escape the OAD-"

Mark's arms snapped out to his sides as he pushed, "We have to go!"

"Leaving so soon?" My cousin immediately went into a defensive stance as Izoles appeared in the doorway. Westyn stuttered, "S-Sir."

"Step aside," Izoles ordered, more poison in his smile than usual. Westyn pleaded, "But-"

"*Step aside.*" Westyn reluctantly did as he was told, bumping into Mark as he backed into the corner of my cot. Trace recoiled, "Get away from me-"

Even Mark cringed at what happened next. I couldn't look away as Trace's eyes widened and blood streamed from his chest. The bloodcurdling scream rippled up my throat, "TRACE!!"

"Jamaica, no!" Mark caught me, and Westyn threw his arm out in front when I launched from my cot. Trace's hand lifted slightly in the form of a sign, and then dropped limp. His muscles slacked, and his lungs emptied. I felt physical pain in my chest as the Emperor ripped the small knife out of Trace. So, when the man started to talk, I squeezed my eyes tight and looked away, tears nearing the brink. "Have you any more doubt of my ruthlessness, Ms. Jamaica?"

"Don't talk to her," Mark snarled.

"How could you?" Westyn broke softly. Emotions whirred through my head, enough that I wanted to cradle it and start rocking. I'd just lost Trace. I'd just *watched* the Emperor...

"You're Matt's son, right?" Mark looked at the boy next to him in surprise. "How do you-?"

"Hit him with *everything*," Westyn emphasized. Without second command, Mark's hand turned into a flamethrower, which the Emperor narrowly dodged. Mark kept it up until Izoles was forced through the door frame. The door slammed and locked on its own, and Mark wheeled on Westyn, "You said he wouldn't find us!"

Westyn sputtered out bits and pieces of words before holding his head and panicking, "We don't have much time before he breaks down that...door..."

The boy calmed down and slowly approached Trace. Mark asserted, "There's nothing we can do-"

"His chest, the cuts- he's healing," Westyn gasped. My cousin dismissed, "He's gone-"

"See for yourself." Mark hesitantly let go of me and came closer. He sucked in a surprised breath as he stopped next to Westyn, blocking my view. I numbly struggled out of bed and teetered over, just in time to see the last of the gash in my boyfriend's side close. A moment later, Trace took a deep breath, sitting up as if he'd just had a nightmare. I squeaked, "Trace?"

He glanced at the three of us, then grabbed at his shirt where the fresh bloodstain was. "He-He stabbed me. I'm dead-"

"You were," Westyn corrected, face still covered in shock, "and somehow, you revived yourself-"

The door shook, Izoles' muffled voice behind it. At Westyn's beckoning, we all followed him as he revealed another door at the back of the room. Trace huffed, "How many secret rooms do you have?!"

"What are you talking about? This is the back door," Westyn replied, "This'll give you a head start. Go find Bruno, get the dragons-"

"You know Bruno?" Mark caught, but Westyn waved it off, "Doesn't matter. You need to get out of here now."

Mark was first out the door, supporting me as I stumbled after him. "Are you gonna make it?"

I determinedly nodded as Trace hopped out behind us. He turned genuinely stating, "Thank you."

Sadness swelled in Westyn's eyes before he closed the door. "I can call Beuti to come get us once they untether her-"

"Why don't we look for Bruno?" Trace suggested. At Mark's glare, he added, "In the meantime. Jamaica can find him, Mark, you know she can."

My cousin looked away a second, wetting his lips. "Jamaica, do you have the energy?"

"I should." I knelt down, laying my hand flat to the concrete. I would have no help from plants, I realized. I would have to stretch my powers out solely on my own strength. So I did, checking each building for Bruno's presence. Just as I began to strain, I picked up on him, sitting in the corner of a cell, alone in the block. I pulled myself in and took a deep breath, taking help from Mark and Trace to stand.

I gave them directions, and we began to sneak across the facility, Mark using his fire whenever we were seen. It didn't take as long as I thought to reach Bruno's location, which I found oddly lacking in guards.

As one of my feet lagged, and I started to trip, Trace caught my arm and put it around his neck in one fluid motion. Mark took the lead, opening the door cautiously and poking his head in.

No one's here.

"I don't care for your company, James," a familiar voice called. The three of us rushed in to see him sitting in the back

130

corner of his cell, elbows on his knees and wrists handcuffed. "Bruno?"

His eyes popped open, and no sooner did he see us, he was on his feet in front of the bars. "Kids- what are you...? I-"

"No, time. We're busting you out," Mark proudly declared. I grabbed a bar, but Mark gently removed it, saying, "Save your energy, J. I'll do it."

Letting go, my cousin turned his hands white hot. Bruno backed away as Mark began to bend bars away from the middle, breaking horizontal beams in the process. By the time he had created a large enough hole and cooled the metal, he was panting, but he still grinned his face off with pride.

Bruno hesitantly approached the hole, saying, "Kids you shouldn't have come."

"We weren't gonna let him take you," Mark insisted, but Bruno adamantly shook his head.

"You should have," he sighed, some of the shock of seeing us wearing off, "You've only seen the surface of James' torment, and I hope that's all you ever experience-"

"Nothing he could do would have stopped us," Trace pressed. He and Mark sounded tackily heroic, but I couldn't agree with them more.

A thunderous roar rippled through the air, making all present glance at the outside door. Mark commented, "Someone just made my dragon very unhappy."

Let's Get Things Straight

16

"We need to leave," Bruno demanded, "It's not safe for us to stay put."

"I'll tell Beuti to come get us," Mark complied. I scoffed, "When has this place ever been safe?"

The blacksmith looked at me, a memory clearly running through his mind. "When my father ran it."

"She's on her way," my cousin informed, melting the links connecting Bruno's cuffs. The man asked, "Are you fit to fly?"

Still caught on the answer about his father, it took me a second to reply, "Uh, yeah. My arm's…fine…"

I knew the Emperor's presence in my head too well, but it didn't mean I could stop the pain coursing through every nerve of my head.

Mugireti…

I'm holding him back, but his power's a lot stronger when he's this close. You need to get out of here.

The ground shook as a dragon landed just outside the door, and Mark ran out to meet her.

On it.

Trace helped me stumble out to Beuti, working with Mark to get me onto the dragon's back. I warned, "Mark, four people is a lot of weight. Are you sure she can handle it?"

He paused before replying, "She said it'll be harder to keep up with the rest of the group, but she'd rather do that than risk leaving someone behind."

Trace was behind me now, and just as Bruno started to climb up Beuti's fore talon, the pain spiked in my head, causing me to throw my skull forward into Mark when I jolted.

"Jamaica-"

Jamaica, I can't fend him off much longer, go!

"Go!" I grunted. Beuti was quick to react, getting herself off the ground seconds after Bruno swung his leg over her spine. But just before we flew over the gates, Mugireti's mental shield wavered again, and it sounded like my mother screaming in my ears as I passed out.

----0----

Even from the back, Bruno immediately saw Jamaica list to the left before Trace caught her. The boy took great care to keep her centered against him, hinting to the smith that she very well may have fainted. As terrible as he felt to think it, he hoped it was due to blood loss from whatever wound had been inflicted on her wrapped arm.

The rest of the team burst from the dragon cells below, soon taking to the air and forming a ring around Beuti with Mugireti in the lead.

The flight was long, stretching well into the night before the group found a comfortable place to land. Bruno dismounted in one swift motion, reaching up to take Jamaica's body from Trace and Mark. "I'll bring her to Mugireti."

As he carried her, Bruno couldn't suppress his thoughts. This poor girl. Only fourteen, and she'd already suffered so much at James' hand. Jamaica was tough and resilient, just like her mother; Bruno knew that. But seeing the scar on one arm and the wrap on the other- it was sickening.

He came close to Mugireti, the dragon curling his head toward his belly in anticipation. "She passed out at the beginning of the flight, but she's still breathing, and her heartbeat is strong. She should be fine."

He laid the girl down next to her giant protector and began to retreat before Mugireti nudged him in the shoulder.

I know about you. I can sense it as well as I do Trace.

Bruno looked away a moment before answering, "Then can I ask you not to tell anyone for now? It's not something I'm ready for these kids to know."

While Mugireti looked hesitant, he nodded, then proceed to wrap his neck over to his rider and let his wing fall to go to sleep.

As the smith walked by William and Garrett, the younger caught him, asking, "Is she alright?"

Bruno patiently reported, "She fainted when we took off, but far as I know, it hasn't raised any red flags for Mugireti yet."

"Are you alright?" Garrett's accent came as he joined the two. Bruno hadn't realized his old fibbing habit was intact until he replied, "Fine."

The aged rider's eyes shouldn't have been able to bore into him so intensely, but he almost had to look away before excusing, "I spent years with my brother's twisted mind. There is very little he can blindside me with."

"That doesn't answer the question," Garrett pressed, "Bruno, if somethin' happened-"

"If something happened, I do believe I have a right to privacy," Bruno cut him off. Seeing that it may have been somewhat harsh, he continued, "I understand your concern. James has little sanity in what he does. But I have no interest in digging up the memories by talking about what he may or may or may not have done this time around. As hard as it is, I need you to respect that."

Garrett ground his jaw before letting a defeated sigh go and nodding, "Try to get some sleep, then."

Will hesitated before returning to Divios, and Bruno could've sworn he saw reluctance to the young man's quiet tongue.

The smith realized his forearm had begun to shake again, forcing him to squeeze it until the muscles calmed. It was a chronic nuisance, even if the scars didn't hurt anymore. His partners back at the workshop were aware of the problem, though he'd never gone into detail about why it happened. No one needed to be exposed to his past, including himself.

Bruno laid down in front of the fire, rubbing a thumb over the ridges on his forearm. He tucked his arm close to keep the scars out of sight before closing his eyes and slipping under.

----0----

I slowly woke to the feeling of something wrapping around my arm.

Don't move, I'm just changing your bandages.

My eyes adjusted to the early sunny morning so I could watch the new mineral wrap curl around my stitched arm. It was surreal almost, seeing such a long cut held together by nothing but thin black floss. It made me kind of happy that I couldn't see my shoulder.

135

"Hey," Trace greeted, as he walked over, "Did you just wake up?"

"Yeah," I mumbled. He sat down crossed legged next to me, watching the wrap move. There was a clear hatred in his eyes, and as I glanced at the stitches again, I whispered, "You couldn't have done anything."

His lips thinned, but he didn't reply. "Alright-"

Mark plunked down next to him, "-I can't believe I have to be the one to say this, but we need to talk."

"I'll give you guys some space-" Mark grabbed Trace's shoulder and pulled him to the ground just as he started to get up. "All three of us. What happened in the infirmary?"

"Mark," I protested, but he barreled through, "We watched him regenerate like a freaking X-Men mutant! Something happened. What did you do, Trace?"

Trace's brow furrowed before he slowly answered, "I don't know...I could feel myself dying. It was this huge, terrifying pain in my chest, everything went black, and...and then it all came back, but nothing hurt. Like I'd only fallen asleep. I thought I was dead."

"You were." I smacked Mark's knee. "He was! But if you're alive now, and your sister is just like you-"

"You're not bringing Jamie into this," Trace folded his arms with a deep scowl. Mark pushed, "If you two can't die-"

He is immortal no more.

"What? You want me to be a target dummy?"

One life is endless, the other is limited.

"I was going to say spy, but if you insist-"

"Both of you shut up." When they turned their attention to me, I tapped my forehead, saying, "Courtney."

He will now continue to age-

Whoa, slow down a minute. What do you mean 'immortal no more'? Since when is Trace immortal?

Every animal whisperer is born with eternal life. Should they, by some means, die, their life force can be renewed but once. However, they do not regain this ability. If Trace were to die again, it would be permanent.

"Jamaica?" The wrap had finished hiding my arm, meaning I was free to flinch away from Trace's concerned hand. Before I could think, I blurted, "How old are you?"

"What?"

"Yeah," Mark added, "If you can't die, how do we know you're really as old as you say you are-?"

"Guys, I'm still fifteen!" Trace huffed, "Just like I was yesterday, just like I will be tomorrow!"

He does not lie. He has not developed his power enough to alter others' perception of his age.

"We don't know that for sure-"

"Yes, we do," I stopped my cousin. I began to explain what Courtney had told me, while her presence slipped away as quietly as it had appeared. "...so, if Trace dies again, that's it for him."

"But Jamie-"

"Bring her up in this one more time and I swear, I will kill you," Trace snapped. Mark had his hand on his sword in a nanosecond, growling, "I dare you to try!"

Noticing the aggressive stances forming, I used my good palm to pop both of them in the back of the skull. "Jamaica-!"

"Seriously-?!"

"I'm sorry, are you two rams? If so, then by all means, please keep butting heads while I figure out how we tell everyone Trace came back from the dead!"

"I don't think we should," Mark argued, "What would we say? 'Hey, Trace got killed, but he's alive again, so we're cool'? That won't go over, Jamaica, not at all."

"Actually, Jamaica," Trace didn't notice Mark's glare, but after a few seconds, he mumbled, "I agree with Mark. Trying to

137

explain it isn't going to be easy to start with. I don't think my father or sister could take it if they found out. That's something that needs to be saved for another day, when things have cooled down."

"Are you sure?" I asked, "This is pretty big-"

"I'm sure." The side of his jaw clenched a little, so I left the matter alone. Besides, another had come to mind, and it wasn't going to be fun bringing it up. Mark sighed, "Well, I guess that settles it-"

"Uh, Mark?" I stopped him, then avoided looking at him, "Trace and I- we actually have something to tell you."

You don't mean-?

Trace we have to, he deserves to know.

"What is it?" He observed our hesitancy with impatience.

Let me take the initial shock.

"Mark," Trace carefully spoke, "You won't believe us, but...we met your dad."

Mark bristled, and I thought he would pounce on Trace. "I didn't think even you could stoop so low."

"Mark-" he turned on me and continued, "And I thought you agreed to drop it! You told him?! Of all people!"

"She didn't have to, Mark!" Trace retorted, "Your dad is the reason I didn't die from the cut in my side-!"

"You're lying," Mark growled teeth bared. I piped up, "He's not. Your dad stitched up my arm, Mark."

"I met him last year, too. He's the only reason I vaguely remembered you guys after the Emperor tried to have me brainwashed," Trace recalled, "I just- didn't know it was him."

"Shut up! Both of you!" my cousin scoffed, hauling himself to his feet. Trace yelled, "Mark, c'mon!"

"Shut. Up."

Mark-

I don't wanna hear anymore, Jamaica-

I can prove it!

Though he was just starting to walk away, he stopped and turned partway back to us. I begged, "Give me a chance to prove it, please."

He glowered a moment before puffing out air and coming back, dropping down onto his butt without a word. "The memory you shared."

He started to say something, but I quickly continued, "Just trust me. You had been excited for your dad to show you an invention. Something that could shock people."

"So?" I shifted, scared to keep going. "Izoles forced him to weaponize it. It turned into the devices that Trace and Joey had."

"And how do you know it was him?" Mark insisted, "How do you know he wasn't-?"

"Because you look like him," Trace reasoned. He wasn't wrong. The more I watched Mark, the more I realized he was a spitting image of his father. I added, "Remember that boy? The one who asked if you were Matt's son?"

He quieted, very clearly remembering it. Trace cautiously explained, "His name is Westyn. He's your father's assistant."

Mark knitted his brow, licking his lips several times before breathing, "He's really alive?"

I nodded encouragingly, only to have him suggest, "We should go back."

"Mark-"

"Maybe we can get him out!"

"Mark, we barely made it out this time," Trace tried, but my cousin demanded, "I thought he was dead! For seven years, I thought he was dead! I want to see him myself-"

"And get yourself killed?" Trace chided. I redirected Mark's growing frustration to me, saying, "Mark, he openly defied the Emperor in front of us. That won't go without punishment, you know that. If you go back right now, he may decide that punishment has to be you."

"No doubt, he's going to count on you finding out and wanting to come back," Trace agreed, "I hate to admit it, but your father is perfect bait. And because of that, the Emperor won't kill him. Not while he has value."

"Then what do you suggest I do?" Mark spat, a hint of panic seeping through, "I can't just forget about him! He's-He's alive, I have to do something-!"

"But not right now," Trace soothed, "Wait for things to cool down. You've got a lot of emotions raging, you need to calm down before you do something you regret-"

"I would not regret going back for my father!" my cousin growled defensively, to which Trace replied, "Not what I meant. You'll regret going back and getting yourself captured, which then takes away your father's use to the Emperor. Going back could put his life in danger as well as yours."

My cousin stared at Trace, and I couldn't help doing the same. I knew he had his insights, and his history had aged him a little, but talking about Mark's father like that made him sound like he'd been through war and come back scarred.

Mark sullenly stood, murmuring, "I should...I should get some more sleep."

He trudged back to Beuti, still curled up with her head under her wing. As I watched, Trace muttered, "I was harsh, wasn't I?"

"You weren't wrong," I offered. He gazed off into space a few moments before his brow creased. "Trace, you and I both know it's dangerous. I would expect you to say the same thing if you saw my mom-"

"It's not that," he brushed off, "We mentioned Westyn knew Mark's dad. Did you happen to get Westyn's last name?"

"What?"

"It's just bugging me," Trace shook his head, "All the times I got captured, I've never seen him, and he looks like he's our age. What's more, he works with Mark's father, and he knows Bruno."

Now that he said that, I did remember him deflecting the possibility of knowing Bruno, and poorly doing so. "You think he knows Bruno?"

"What if Bruno knows him?" Trace thought. I disagreed, "Bruno is the Emperor's brother, he could easily be well known throughout the OAD."

"We should still ask him," he insisted, "This kid works for the Emperor and he's no older than me."

The fear flickering through his eyes made me understand that this was important to him. Maybe I didn't get why, but the last thing I wanted to see was Trace afraid.

"Let me ask him then," I volunteered, "He might be more open with me."

He nodded and continued to stare out at our quiet sleeping group. I looked down at his hand, and it sparked a memory. "What were you about to say?"

"I wasn't," he replied, glancing back over. I clarified, "Not now. Right before Izoles- when he- you know..."

His eyes drifted to his shoes. "You formed your hand like you were going to sign something. What was it?"

Reluctantly, he murmured, "I thought I wouldn't get to say it."

"Say what?" He raised his hand with index, pinkie, and thumb extended, and shifted it back and forth twice. "What does that mean?"

He swallowed, looking like he was building up courage. "I love you."

My body stiffened up as my eyes widened, so he began excusing, "I knew I was gonna die in a few seconds, it was impulsive. I'm sorry, I shouldn't have-"

141

"You…you thought that?" I gasped, "You were dying, and you thought that?"

He hesitated a little, then guiltily confessed, "It was the only thing I thought. It's weird, I know, and it shouldn't have crossed my mind, but-"

"Trace," I smiled, blushing so much I tucked my chin down, "I love you, too."

"Don't say it unless you mean it," he warned. He was curling in on himself, I could see that. But how could he think I didn't mean it? "Look, you're fourteen and I'm fifteen. People say we don't really know what love is at this age. I shouldn't have signed it, I'm sorry."

He started to get up, so I blurted, "Then we wait."

Our eyes met, and I felt my stomach float up at the dark blue of his irises. "So maybe we don't know what love is now. We know what it means."

"That doesn't help," he worried. I pushed, "At some point in the future, we'll know what it is, won't we?"

He broke eye contact, cautiously inquiring, "And what if it's not what we have?"

"We won't know unless we stick it out, right?" I dared. I touched his hand and assured, "I think we do have it. And it's obvious you do too. But if you're worried about us being wrong, it's okay. We're young. Just don't give up on us so fast, alright? You made a bold move, that's all."

There was a pause between us, and then I caught the half smirk, "Give up on you? I don't think I could if I tried."

I grinned and pulled him into a hug, which he returned, saying, "You're right. We don't know where we are yet, but that shouldn't stop us. And if you're willing to keep going, so am I."

After establishing that we were still on the same page, we sat against Mugireti's stomach, taking in the fresh air and sunlight as the others slowly began to wake. I kept a careful eye on Mark, seeing him more antisocial than usual. I wished we could've broken the news to him easier, playing different scenarios through my head of what Trace and I could've done differently. Beuti touched her nose to his arm several times, and each time, he accepted the comfort, but it didn't seem to make him feel any better.

Are you okay?

There was a long silence, and I started to think he wouldn't answer, even if my question had gotten to him. But his emotions drifted over as his answer. He was a thousand and one kinds of upset, from extreme sadness, to intense anger, to overwhelming fear. But somehow, my guilt got through all that, because after a few seconds, he replied.

I get it. I can't go back. I just...after so many years of accepting that he was dead...after so many years missing someone who could never be there...it makes me feel like a little kid all over again. I can't explain how bad I want to see him, J.

My mind flickered over to my mom before quickly snapping back, but it was too late. His emotions had focused into an epiphany.

Oh.

After an awkward pause, he seemed to calm down, storm receding into a neutral cloud.

You really think she's alive?

It's only an instinct. But I'm just so sure, Mark, you have to believe me-

I- Maybe. You saw my father-

And talked to him.

And...talked to him. That's proof.

He stopped when my hurt struck him.

Jamaica, I wanna believe you-

But you don't believe what you don't see.

It was a bitter jab, I admit it. But I thought that with his father proven alive, he'd at least be willing to humor the idea of

143

my mom. She was there, I knew it. Izoles was the one making her scream. Her scream...

Her scream was louder.

Wha-?

I hear her scream whenever I pass out, remember?

Yeah-

It was louder this time, Mark. When we were leaving, it was so loud, it was practically in my ears. The volume changes depending how far we are from the OAD-

Izoles is messing with your head-

But why use the scream every single time? He wants me to think about her, Mark-

J, he's rubbing salt in your wound-

But why?

He paused, so I pushed on.

Why remind me of it? Yes, I get defensive, I get mad. But he uses different approaches if that's what he wants from us. The scream seems- I don't know- it just seems too repetitive for him.

Well, if he's got nothing else to use...

I suppose my dejection got a little too strong, because his sympathy seeped into my head.

If you're absolutely certain, I'll try out a little faith. But don't expect me to follow blindly. You need to make sure you have a reality check from time to time.

Mark understood that my silence meant I was done with the conversation, so he quietly retreated from my head.

Jamaica? We're going to head out soon, now that almost everyone's up.

Okay.

Are you alright?

When I didn't answer, Mugireti nudged me. Trace noticed, but chose to observe instead of saying anything. I stroked my dragon's right eye ridge, muttering, "Mark still doesn't think there's any chance Mom is alive."

For some, it takes a long time to base a hope on hope's sake. If he doesn't come around, you still have Trace and me.

144

I nodded unconvincingly. Was is it too much to ask that my own cousin trust me?

Everyone was up soon after, those who had still been fast asleep getting their faces drenched by some of Garrett's water (to which he promptly blamed K.C. with a slight smile). Trace mounted Mugireti behind me, pulling Jamie up behind him. As she swung a leg over Mugireti's spine, she continued to blearily wring her wet hair out.

Is everyone ready?

Once Mugireti got the all clear from his passengers and the other dragons, he was the first to take to the sky. The dragons flew in tight formation, wind rushing by endlessly. Somewhere during the flight, I must've fallen asleep, because I suddenly found myself peering in on a very tense situation.

A Little Bit of Rest

17

Matt and Westyn stood in the throne room, no guards to be seen. The man was calm, a little annoyed, even, but the boy was stilled with fear. Matt noticed this, though he made no move to reassure his assistant.

"You are aware that there are consequences in this facility, yes?" The Emperor paced in front of the two, a scornful smile on his face. Matt's eyes followed him with a hatred only deepened by time, but Westyn insisted on staring straight forward. Matt answered, "In six years, I have been nothing but loyal, despite our deal having been neutralized."

"Yes, you mentioned that at the time of the incident," the Emperor agreed, "but you see, it was not loyalty to me that caused you to stay. You are a family-oriented man, Mr. Frelck, are you not?"

"I am," he muttered. His boss continued, "Then it would make absolute sense that you worked under me without question that first year. But in the years after, that motivator disappeared. So, in order to stay so long, you would have needed motivation just as potent."

"If you would, Sir, please be blunt," Matt huffed, folding his arms. Izoles passed him for maybe the third time, saying, "Your son was not the only member of your family you felt a need to protect. Like everyone else, you thought your sister-in-law was dead, until you saw her again for yourself."

Matt's jaw settled as his glare intensified. "Don't pretend and tell me you showed loyalty based only on the sake of good will. You make your choices for your loved ones-"

"And one of those choices was remaining here," Mark's father retorted, "I gave up a life with my wife and my son to take care of another's wife, another's son. I let them believe I was dead in order to stay here."

"You think they believe you dead?" Izoles laughed. Matt let a little confusion slip, and Izoles continued, "You think after your niece has met you, she won't convince your son? After all, she has a stubborn mind like her mother. And if she convinces him, what's to stop him from convincing his mother? Very soon they will both know you didn't die. What emotional stress might that cause, I wonder? Anger? Hatred? *Betrayal*?"

"I did not betray them," Matt, defensively growled. The Emperor agreed, "Oh no, of course not. But that will not stop them from questioning why you deceived them. What's more, what message do you send your son, working for the man who wants him dead?"

The Emperor stopped in front of my uncle, whose jaw had gone still.

"Defy me again, and you will be the cause of their demise." The two stared each other down for several seconds before Matt finally broke eye contact. "I understand, Sir. It will not happen again."

"See to that. You won't get another warning." Matt began to leave, but turned a moment. "Westyn, when you are done here, if you are able, please assist me in the Infirmary. Several men need fresh bandages. They were in- they were near the explosion."

Westyn didn't answer, standing rigid as a statue. But during the conversation, his eyes had shifted down, eyebrows inched together. The Emperor stopped in front of him and scolded, "Do you have anything to say for yourself?"

He spoke so soft, I almost didn't catch it when he mumbled, "You killed him."

Izoles' hand shot out, and he gripped Westyn's jaw, commanding, "Louder."

"You killed him," Westyn growled, braving to look up at his boss. Izoles shook him by the face, barking, "Louder!"

"You killed him!" the boy screamed, pulling out of his elder's hold, "You killed him when he didn't even stand a chance!"

"Westyn, shut up, you'll get in trouble!" I hissed, hoping somehow he would hear me. But he just kept going, "He was defenseless and critically injured, and it wasn't fair-!"

"My intention is not to be fair!" Izoles yelled, but the medical assistant shouted over him, "You killed him! I HATE YOU-!!"

It was like watching a time lapse video of fluid movement. The Emperor pulled his arm to the ready and backhanded Westyn across the cheek. I jumped and covered my mouth with both hands as Westyn hit the ground like a plank. Within seconds, there was a burning red mark on his face. "Get up."

Westyn lay there curled tightly, fists balled and tears forming in his eyes. "Get up!"

The Emperor grabbed him by the arm and threatened, "Learn your place, Westyn. Or I will teach it to you."

And that set something off in me. Some level of anger that I'd never thought possible. I found myself snarling, "Why don't *you* go die in a ditch!"

I swung a fist-

"Gack!" Too late, I realized I had woken up, and Trace keeled over from the punch that had landed squarely in his stomach. It was still daytime, and the dragons were on the ground.

"Whoa, take it easy there, J!" K.C. snorted as she walked up. Trace agreed through staggered breaths, "I know I screw up-sometimes, but…could you give me a warning? Or at least- a chance- to fix it?"

"Sorry, that wasn't meant for you," I apologized, mind still on what I'd just witnessed. When he got his wind back, he questioned, "Not for me?"

My boyfriend and cousin both took on looks of worry as Trace cautiously asked, "Are you alright?"

"The Emperor, he-he had Matt and Westyn in a room, he was reprimanding them-"

"Matt and Westyn?" K.C. asked. Trace quickly dismissed, "We'll explain in a second. What happened?"

"He sent Matt off with a threat, but Westyn- he slapped him. He hit him hard enough that he fell over, Trace. There was this big red mark on his cheek, and the Emperor was telling him to get up- I woke up before I could see anything else. Trace what if he gets hurt? What if he gets…?"

I couldn't push the k word off my tongue, but he understood what I was aiming for. K.C. did too, chewing on her lower lip. "Who are they?"

Trace explained who Matt was, only to rein K.C. back in from her shock, surprise, and excitement. "This is just crazy! My uncle is really alive? Mark's dad is still alive?"

"Yes, he is, and how he's stayed alive this long is a mystery. Now Westyn," he saw that he had her attention again, "we don't know much about him. Just that he's Matt's assistant, and he's about our age."

"And you said the Emperor slapped him?" my cousin asked me. I glanced away, confirming, "Hard enough to hit the floor. It's gonna leave a nasty bruise, I know it."

"And to think, I was coming over here to suggest we try to negotiate with the Emperor," she muttered. Trace's eyes zeroed in on her. "You what? That's insane."

"Is it? If we could get him off our backs, if we could get our families out of danger, wouldn't you want to try?"

"Of course I would, but I've known the Emperor a lot longer than you. Negotiating with him is a death wish." She

149

adjusted to bite more of her lip. Trace caught on faster this time that he was snapping and backed down, "If I thought there was a chance, I would say go for it. But he is ruthless. No amount of compromise is going to stop him from getting what he wants, which is you three dead."

She nodded solemnly.

Don't worry.

She didn't react, so I just sat in silence. "I don't want anyone else getting hurt because of us."

She stood and shuffled away towards Pirsniketi. Trace huffed, "I really need to stop making your cousins hate me."

"She'll be okay," I assured, though maybe not convincingly enough. Mugireti snaked his head to us, nuzzling my shoulder.

You're up.

How long was I asleep?

Trace said you passed out about halfway through the flight yesterday, and you slept through the night.

Oh.

C'mon, we're s'posed to be back in the air soon. Garrett says Bruno's been a bit anxious.

Bruno, anxious? Before I knew what I was doing, I got up and wandered through camp, Trace trailing behind. "Jamaica, where are you going?"

"Where's Bruno?" I asked, continuing to search. Before my boyfriend could answer, I saw Bruno leaning against Mescheaf's chest and throat, stroking the underside of her jaw with his right hand. His left arm lay across his stomach. The closer I got, it looked more like he was firmly pressing it in. Had his brother hurt him? "Jamaica-"

"Go wait by Mugireti," I whispered to Trace, "I wanna talk to him alone."

He hesitated, but went back to my dragon. I strode up to the blacksmith and forced out the chirp, "Hey, Bruno."

He and Mescheaf looked up, his hand pausing. "Jamaica."

Mescheaf shifted her head away so he could stand, and a second later, I was being checked over. "You passed out during the flight yesterday, are you alright-?"

"I'm fine," I replied softly, "Are you?"

"Of course, why wouldn't I be?" he returned, still concerned for me. I hugged my wrapped arm gently, explaining, "The dragons are talking. Garrett says you're anxious."

His jaw clenched, and he looked away towards Mescheaf's right wing, partially extended so that it touched the ground. "Now what would give him that idea?"

Mescheaf drew her head back and tucked it under the wing. A few more seconds passed before I got up the courage to inquire, "Do you know Westyn?"

"What?" his sight whipped back to me, and he stared as if I couldn't have asked that question. I backtracked, "There was a boy there, around my age. His name is Westyn. He knew who you were, so…I thought maybe you knew him."

His jaw moved a little before he shook his head, denying, "I'm sorry. I don't. Though I fear for his safety, if he is under my brother's power."

It was an obvious lie, I could tell. But I decided it was best not to dig. He looked worn out, and it seemed like Garrett was right.

Bruno suddenly took me by the shoulders and pushed me over to Mescheaf's chest, hurriedly telling me to sit down. "Bruno-"

"Get Mugireti's attention. Now." The stark authority in his voice startled me, but he held up my left wrist. Even under the wrap, it was glowing gold.

Mugireti. He's-

A sharp pang racketed through my skull, and I hunched over to hold my head. Bruno caught me just I tipped to the side, yelling for someone, anyone, to be up.

Mugireti!

151

"C'mon, kiddo, stay with me," Bruno whispered, squeezing my shoulder. My head throbbed harder and harder, and I let out a cry, trying to release the pain.

Mugireti, please!

I'm trying! He's blocking me!

Tears streamed down my face, Bruno trying to keep my attention while his brother tried to kill me from the inside out. And then, my skull suddenly got more crowded.

Jamaica, I'm through! I'm through! Just relax, I can take care of it!

I relaxed as much as I could, and screamed as the pain got worse. Mugireti was my only shield now, pushing and shoving to force the Emperor out of my head. My eyesight blurred, and when the pain finally began to dull, so did my consciousness. I finally went out like a light when I heard my mother's scream...

K.C. limped through the OAD and finally collapsed with no one to defend her. Trace and Mark were fighting, and Mark crumbled. Two headstones with the same name. Knives, swords, so much blood- and suddenly the scenes just cracked. Almost like a TV screen shattering away into a void. Nervous, I stepped through the jagged hole in the middle, into the nothingness. Perhaps I'd expected something, but all I got was the urge to wake up.

"Wake up...wake up... c'mon!" I let out a groan of frustration.

Jamaica?

Mugireti's voice thundered around me, as if hooked up to invisible speakers. "Mugireti?"

Jamaica!

There was a huge flush of relief from both of us, and I insisted, "Where are you? Where am I?"

His presence seemed to deflate, so I pushed, "Mugireti?"

A foggy mist formed in front of me, condensing into a picture of me in a hospital bed. There were wires connected to me, and an oxygen mask over my face. My dad sat in front of one of

152

the few machines around me, still and unmoving with his head in his hands. Now very aware of my own heart thudding in my chest, I asked again, "Mugireti...where am I?"

You've been in the hospital for two days now. Trace said...the doctors told your father you're in a coma.

"No...no, that can't be right. The Emperor attacked me again, but..." I stared at my dad, impulsively reaching out. I had to be alright. We'd lost Mom, I was all he really had-

My hand went through the image, and I suddenly heard sounds of the hospital. I jerked it back, and everything went silent. Dad stirred, looking over at me. His eyes were red, and my chest tightened.

What happened? You did something, I felt it.

"I-I just touched the image you're showing. My hand went through it, but I could hear the hospital."

Do it again. Try climbing through.

Mugireti's voice was short about it, anxious almost. So, I stuck my hand in, hearing it all once more. I closed my eyes and tried to mimic the motions of climbing into something. I got the sense that I was floating a moment before resting on my back. A soft platform met me underneath, along with a loud beeping in my ear. I groaned and opened my eyes, blearily taking in the walls and ceiling of the room. Mugireti's suggestion had worked.

"Jamaica?" Dad whispered, slowly rising from his seat. I hissed, "Dad."

He picked up my torso and brought me into a tight embrace, adjusting and readjusting as he tried to hold as much of me as possible. His chest heaved as he sobbed, the sounds of heartache coming out right next to my ear.

----0----

It took a few days for the hospital to clear me, and my dad practically never left my side. In that time, I was tested on my everything, from motor functions and mental processing, to any signs of physical damage in my head. I also got bombarded by family and friends relieved to hear that I was awake. Mark and K.C. nearly knocked me flat on the tile of a hallway when they first got to see me. Garrett and Will both suffocated me in hugs, while the blacksmiths audibly fought for the phone when they called. But Trace reacted differently to everyone else.

I was almost done with a session testing my mobility when I noticed him standing outside the room. He waited until I was left alone to hesitantly enter. I joked, "Where've you been? Did the message not reach you?"

"No i-it did." When he stayed huddled by the doorframe, I gently nudged, "Trace? What is it?"

His eyes finally met mine fully, and I saw all the emotions he couldn't hide. I opened my arms up, and he immediately took the offer, wrapping his arms around me and mumbling, "I didn't want to come here and lose you too."

I returned the hug, only now realizing what it must have meant for him to have to come back to the hospital so soon.

We stood like that for a few seconds before someone cleared their throat behind Trace. He jumped away from me when he saw Dad. "Sir, I was just-just-"

"Trace, you're alright. If you weren't, I wouldn't have waited in the hall to give you two your moment." My boyfriend and I both blushed, and my father suppressed a chuckle before explaining, "I actually came to talk to Jamaica about- several things."

"Can Trace stay?" I quickly asked. My father blanked a moment before complying, "Sure."

Trace and I sat on my hospital bed while Dad pulled up a chair in front of us. We listened quietly as he told us about Mom, and about Uncle Matt. "Dad, we know all of this."

His lips pursed. "Last year, you told me you fought him. And what I'm not sure you understand is why he let you live."

I glanced away, not wanting to think about that memory. "I know I'm the third of a line to try and defeat him. He called me an opportunity."

My father's jaw clenched, and he took a moment to compose himself. Once he could keep his voice even, he spoke, "He knows you're not ready. He knows it will take several years before you're skilled enough to fight him without his holding back. He more than likely believes the proper age will be the same as when he killed Courtney. The Emperor is waiting, Jamaica, waiting until you're her age. And when you reach it- I can't say what kind of hell may be unleashed."

Trace squeezed my hand as I gaped, no doubt feeling the same shock I did. My eyes drifted down to my arm. I was told doctors had swarmed to get it professionally cleaned and wrapped, and were amazed at the quality of the stitches done by someone outside of the medical field. I'd been just as surprised as them when I found out the wound had been cauterized. Nonetheless, the doctors still told me to take it easy while the cuts healed, and when the time was right, to start rehabilitating my arm to its full use.

"Then I'll just have to train harder," I found myself saying. Dad started to protest, so I continued, "He wants to kill me whether I'm ready or not. My arm proves that. Why shouldn't I prepare myself to fend him off-?"

A knock on the door caught our attention. A doctor stood there with a clipboard, wondering if now was a good time to interrupt. Dad welcomed him in. "Well, Ms. Zwivelle, your test results have come back, and you are a very lucky young lady. The only physical damage we could find were the scar and the laceration on your arms, and otherwise, your mental processing and motor functions are right where they should be. I've filled out the release forms. Whenever you're ready, you're free to go."

"Thank you very much, Doctor," my dad replied, standing to shake the man's hand. His smile was tight in a way that clued me in on the fact that his mind was occupied with other thoughts than my discharge. Trace squeezed my hand again, and I looked down at my toes.

When I got home, Dragon tried and succeeded to tackle me, and Pashince took it upon himself to give me a thorough search

155

over to make sure nothing was wrong. But even with these distractions, I kept thinking about Dad. I kept thinking about him even as I lay against Mugireti's belly later that day, basking in the patches of sunlight filtering through the canopy.

He's your father, it's natural that he doesn't want you to be in danger.

I know, but he knows the dangers of my life. He knows I can't avoid them.

But it is still his instinct as a parent to want to protect you. You're his child, his only child at that. Imagine what it must be like for him having to let you go without knowing if you'll ever come back.

I suppose he was right. I worried myself about my dad being left alone if something ever happened to me. Why was it so hard to accept that he feared for my safety? "Hey, you coming to practice?"

Trace trotted to a stop in front of me. It looked like he'd made a beeline from the house. I denied, "I doubt Dad will let me. I just got out of the hospital, after all-"

"I reasoned with him," Trace bobbed his head to the side. My eyebrows rose. "How much stuttering did that take?"

"Shut up," he smiled, batting my good shoulder, "C'mon. He said if you sit and watch for the first few days, you can come."

Practice and Practice and Practice

18

"Scar duck-! Ooh!" I cringed. She had been chasing after Jamie during practice, and hadn't noticed Garrett until he clotheslined her. I was guilty of trying not to laugh as she fell flat on her back, and then refused Garrett's hand to help her up. When he knelt to talk to her though, she suddenly pounced on him. For a second, it worked, and he went over backwards. But what Scarlet forgot was that Garrett was much stronger than her. He easily lifted her off him and pinned her with a single hand despite her wild struggling. Despite other people sparring nearby, I heard him under the noise saying, "Gettin' better, but you're not quite there yet, kid."

"How you holding up?" Trace asked, plunking down next to me on the step in front of the workshop's door. I replied with sarcasm, "Well, my arm isn't brain numbingly painful."

I saw his smile sag, so I continued, "I really just wish I could join practice. Will and Garrett won't even let me go to ability training until my dad clears me."

"At least you have ability practice," he tried, "All I can do is try to teach Jamie myself. And so far- it hasn't gone very well."

I creased my brow, so he continued, "She doesn't have the patience for the headaches that come with letting all the surrounding thoughts in, so she keeps shutting the ability out entirely. I can't figure out how to help her focus on one of the voices, or how to only let one in at a time. I'm not even sure how I did it, growing up."

"Hm," I thought, "That's a tough one."

Then an idea popped in my head, and I asked, "You guys practice in the workshop, right?"

"We go into the room with the statues," Trace nodded, "It's the quietest."

"Can I come with you today?"

"Why, so you can watch me fail to teach my sister?" he huffed. "No. I have an idea that may help."

He glanced out at practice. Jamie had teamed up with Scarlet, and Garrett was fighting both of them. "I'm open to suggestions."

He stayed with me to observe the practice grounds, and for a few minutes, we said nothing. Then, he spoke up again, "Jamica, the scars you've gotten over the years- would you trade any of them away?"

"What?"

"Your scars. Would you get rid of them if you could?"

"Why do you ask?" he absent mindedly played with his fingers before mumbling, "When I- you know…came back to *life*- it didn't just heal my wounds. All my scars are gone, my skin is a blank slate. And I just- I haven't felt like me lately. My scars are like a map of my history, but now they've been erased. It feels wrong, Jamica, it just-"

At this point, he couldn't push out any more of a description, setting his forehead in his palm. I placed my hand on his shoulder and tried to comfort, "Well, with how our lives are, you're sure to earn more soon enough."

He looked at me, and I quickly took it back, "Sorry. There's no good way to phrase that, is there?"

And then he burst out laughing. The butterflies in my stomach had a dance festival, as always, when I heard that sound. I couldn't even get him to tell me what about my bad assurance had made him laugh, but I loved to hear it anyway.

----0----

Once sparring practice had ended, I followed Jamie and Trace into the Statue Room. Jamie dragged her feet, whining, "But this hopeless! And useless. Why are we even doing this anymore?"

"You need to learn, Jamie," Trace insisted, "The sooner you can control your powers, the sooner you can use them."

"I'm not even good at it," she grumbled. I offered, "It takes time."

"You guys had time. I don't," she argued, "Why are you even coming with us today? Aren't you supposed to go with Garrett and Will?"

Trace shot me an apologetic look, then explained to his sister, "Jamaica's not allowed to join any physical practice until her dad says it's okay."

"Okay, but why is she coming with us?" I narrowed my eyes at her, and decided to try something.

To help you.

"But I don't want help, I don't even want to do this," she moaned as we reached the doors of the room. Trace confusedly asked, "What?"

As a satisfied smile slipped onto my face, his gaze turned smug. "You didn't."

"I did," I grinned. Jamie looked back and forth between us. "What's wrong with you two?"

I locked eyes with her and pointedly pressed my lips together.

Nothing.

159

Her eyes grew wide. "But you don't- you're not an animal whisperer!"

"A what?" I giggled. She continued, "That's what Bruno called us. Animal whisperers. And you aren't one."

Trace shook his head, teeth peering out between his lips as he led the way into the Statue Room. "No, she's not, but she has telepathy like we do."

We sat in the middle of the room, and Trace said, "Well, if you have any ideas…"

I turned to Jamie. She was still pouting, arms crossed tightly over her chest. "Jamie, reach out to me."

She did as she was told, just not how I expected. I got popped in the nose by the back of her hand, followed by a not very sympathetic sorry. "Not what I meant. Okay, reach out with your mind."

"I've tried listening for Trace's voice before, everything else just floods in-"

"I'm not asking you to listen for me," I clarified, "I'm telling you to actively aim your thoughts at me."

Sss…tupi…stupi…dd…stupid…

Me or the exercise?

She popped an invisible eyebrow in my direction, so I shrugged.

Consst…sst…ellaa…

She grunted in frustration, so I asked, "What are you having trouble with?"

"There's too much static in your head. I can't break through," she puffed, "Why are you thinking about your dad so much?"

I hadn't realized I was. But before I could say so, Trace stopped her, "Jamie, that's really not something you can ask."

"Why not?"

"It's that society thing I told you about."

"Society is stupid if I'm not allowed to ask why someone's worrying so much about their dad."

"Jamie-"

160

She folded her arms stubbornly as his eyes widened in surprise. His face set to argue, only to have his eyes squeeze shut and his hands cup around his ears. "Would you cut that out?"

She picked her chin up as if to say, *make me*, which based on his facial expression after that, she probably did. Trace glanced over at me.

I'm gonna regret letting you teach her that method. I just know it.

"Can I go now?" Jamie impatiently piped up, watching the two of us. Trace smirked, "You can go *practice*."

She let out a sound that lay somewhere between a no and a goat bleating as she fell backwards. Trace and I couldn't help cracking up, and I could see the smile she tried so hard to hide.

----0----

I got hit in the back with a rush of water, and just as I started to get my bearings, the water circled around and washed over me from the front, knocking me to my back. As it shot down from overhead, I finally threw my arms up crossed to send a shield of air around me, just so I could get a staggered breath in. My left arm faltered, and the water ended up crashing across my face and chest. Just before it could attack again, I shouted, "Uncle, uncle! I give!"

As I panted and tried to get a decent breath in, Garrett appeared next to me to help me up. "Your pa really shouldn't a' kept you outta practice for two weeks. Your reflexes are startin' to slow down."

As he pulled me to my feet, I complained, "Says the rider who still has use of both his arms. The doctor agrees with my dad that I need to heal more before I can even think of rehabilitation."

"This is one a' the cases where I know a bit more than a doctor," Garrett cynically replied, "and Bernard, bless his heart, the chicken-shit- my apologies, language, I know. But he knows damn well better than this."

He started to fiddle with the hilt of his knife, so I pushed, "What do you mean?"

There was a still pause before he asked, "He never has told you, has he?"

At my confused look, Garrett sighed, "Your parents met when they were teenagers, only a few years older than you. Didn't take long before her secret was out. Squirt, he knows a lot more 'bout riders than he lets on, and the only reason he's actin' otherwise is because of Anita."

"Because of…Mom?" I repeated, somewhat uncomfortable. "Yes, because of your…"

He picked up on my discomfort, stopping himself from ranting. "You know I love your pa to pieces, same as I did your mama. But after what happened to her, he's so scared a' losin' you, he's forgettin' that you're a rider. Injuries aren't something we worry about like other people do."

"But I need to heal-"

"I know you do. But ya need to practice while you heal, or you start to lose what you learn. Will and I are still gettin' back up to par to where we used to be, and we've been doin' this for years-"

"Hey guys!" K.C. yelled over, "Are you coming back to practice?"

"Don't get your feathers in a ruffle, squirt!" Garrett yelled back, he turned to me, "Keep this between us if you will? Even if I don't agree, I know your pa's tryin' his best, and I wouldn't want you judgin' him for it."

I nodded and followed him back to Will and my cousins. And just as we returned- I registered seeing Mark's hand fly out from behind him, and orange light. I ducked down as fire flourished over me, afterwards glowering, "I prefer to be alive, you know!"

"It was a joke," Mark stuck his tongue out, "I don't actually want you half-baked any more than you do."

"C'mon, you two, settle down," Will smiled, "Now, I assume you've all gathered by now that today's lesson is to know

162

your surroundings. The chances are that in the OAD, you'll be fighting upwards of three- or four-to-one at any given time. Generally the reason you want to avoid fighting at all, if you can. Therefore, you not only need to be aware of where your opponents are, but also what your teammates are doing."

"So, what? We fight you guys and hope we don't hit each other?" K.C. guessed. Will leaned into an attack stance. "Precisely."

K.C. and I dove sideways to avoid the jets of fire that flew from his palms, while Mark stood his ground to take the blow. I stayed low as K.C. swung a spray of water wide to distract Will, though it got Mark too. "K.C.!"

"Not intentional!" I cracked the earth under Garrett's feet before he could get his aim straight to hit her with more flames, and saw Mark pull his arms back for something. I felt wind barrel toward us, and the air warmed up- "Jamaica, move!"

I didn't react quick enough to the warning and got knocked forward onto my stomach, a scream stuck in my throat. It felt like my back was burning.

I heard curses from Garrett and Mark panicking as everyone ran over. "Damn it, her pa's gonna have me for this-"

"Oh my god, I hit her, I hit her, oh my-"

"Mark, calm down, she'll be alright-"

"Her whole back is burned-"

"K.C.-" As Will continued to try and calm my cousins, Garrett whispered, "Hey, you're alright, just stay still, stay still-"

A layer of water rolled over my back, and though it stung at first, a cooling sensation came in moments. "I'll take her back to Bernard, see if he has aloe. Either keep teachin' 'em, or take them home."

Garrett gently picked me up and I winced as he rolled me onto my back in his arms. "You're okay, squirt, you're okay..."

He kept murmuring reassurances as he carried me through the woods and up the hill to my house. Mugireti opened one sleepy eye as we passed, and then clambered to his feet.

What happened?!

163

Mark- accident-

"I'll tell ya in a minute, Mugireti, lemme get her to Bernard first," Garrett told my dragon. When he reached the front door, he kicked the bottom corner, calling out, "Bernard, open up, it's an emergency!"

Whether Dad heard that or not above Dragon's barking, I didn't know. But the cooling effect of the water was starting to wear off where Garrett's arm was placed under my back.

The door opened, Dad restraining Dragon by nothing but the collar, and Garrett strode in, going straight for the dining room. As he lay me down on the table and rolled me back onto my stomach, my dad exclaimed the same two words Mugireti had. Garrett waved it off with his hand and said, "Accident durin' practice. Do you have aloe?"

"Of course, I- Garrett, what happened?"

"Get me aloe," the rider sternly ordered. Dad let go of the dog and yanked our refrigerator door open, pulling a bottle of green slime out. "I let her go back to practice for one day-"

"Bernard, shut up," Garrett snapped, slowly evaporating the water. Dad's voice, as rare occasion would have it, began to raise in volume as he protested, "No, damn it, she is my daughter-!"

"And this ain't a conversation we'll have when she can hear us," I heard my mentor growl through his teeth, "Now help me spread the aloe."

My back felt numb and cold as the two silently covered my back in the ooze, carefully lifting my shirt away. When they were almost done, I finally muttered, "Dad?"

"Hey, sweetheart. Are you okay?"

"Yeah." I wanted to tell them not to fight, but I could feel the tension. It was going to happen, and I couldn't stop it. "Don't lose your relationship. Mom wouldn't want it."

I felt like I was playing a guilt card, using Mom, but I didn't know what else to do. I knew they were going to fight, and if neither of them was grounded, who knows how far they might go.

164

The two steadily left the room once they finished covering my back. It still hurt, but now it was at least bearable. No sooner did the door close, I heard my dad hiss, "Garrett, this was reckless, even for you-"

"She has got to keep up with her team-"

"At what expense?! Garrett, she's fourteen, you can't expect her to put the weight of the world on her shoulders-!"

"You think I have a choice?! Or don't you remember what it was like when it was us fightin' him-?"

"It isn't us fighting him anymore, *Garrett*," Dad said more aggressively, "Though if you really want to go back to that, maybe I should remind you that I almost lost both of them when Jamaica was only five! And I nearly lost my daughter again less than a month ago!"

"Bernard, she is a rider, you know she's stronger than that-"

"She isn't even in high school yet, and already she's going to have scars down her arms! Garrett, please," Dad's voice weakened, "I've already lost Anita. So have you, and so has Will. Do you really want to take that chance of losing Jamaica, too?"

There was a long pause before Garrett's calmer voice replied, "No. I don't. But if this cycle continues, and she survives long enough to grow up, the responsibility will fall on one a' her kids. Bernard, it has to end at some point."

"She's just a kid."

"I know," Garrett sighed, in a way that I could just imagine his hands on his hips with his head hung, "I would never a' wished this on her so young, and the fact that he's doin' this now is a horror. That bein' said, I get you wantin' to protect her. But it's my job as her mentor to teach her how to defend herself and use her power to her full extent. Same as her cousins. Accidents like this are gonna happen until their bond is strong enough to work as one. And even if she's injured, the longer she's away from practice, the longer it's gonna take, meanin' the longer we run the risk a' more accidents like this."

There was another hold of silence before Dad asked, "What did happen?"

"Will and I were teachin' them to be aware of their surroundings. Mark blew a hot wind through, tried to warn her- guess she didn't hear him in time. The air went right across her back."

A worried sigh left my dad, and I imagined him retreating into himself to think. I slowly pushed myself off the table and moved over to the door. Dragon, who had lain down on the kitchen's linoleum, scrambled up to accompany me. "How long do you think it'll take for her to heal? She doesn't heal as fast as Anita did."

"She's also younger than when you knew Anita. The power could just be comin' in late. If it does, I give her a week. If not- probably closer to three."

"And I assume you want her in practice regardless," Dad huffed, the sound of a couch cushion squish reaching through the door. Garrett only replied, "I'll take it easy on her."

I opened the door, and both men looked over as Dragon weaseled her way through the opening. It only took a moment for them to realize how much I'd heard, so Garrett promptly excused, "Imma head out. Bernard- at least consider what I said."

And with that, he gave Dragon an affectionate scratch behind the ear and left.

Damaged

19

"Jamaica!" Jamie came running up to me, demanding, "You have to teach me that trick again, you have to!"

"What?"

"Sorry, I tried to stop her," Trace apologized, catching up to his little sister. It was practice time once again, and this time, Dad didn't hold me back. Jamie grabbed my hand and begged, "C'mon, c'mon!"

She suddenly stuck her tongue out at Trace's exasperated face. He groaned and told her, "You know, just because you *can* say things telepathically, doesn't mean you *should*."

"Well just because you can gush about *Jamaica*, doesn't mean you should," she shot back. His cheeks reddened as I snorted, "Seems like you're doing just fine with that little trick."

"Trace is my brother, he doesn't count." I resisted laughing at the expression my boyfriend hid behind his hand. "You know, Dad left me in charge of you. Don't think I won't sit you in front of multiplication tables."

She whipped around. "You don't have the nerve."

"*And* laundry." Now it was her turn to look indignant, and Trace instinctively started to cover his ears at whatever she mentally decided to attack him with. I finally giggled, "Trace, it's fine, I can help her."

He gave me an unsure eyebrow as Jamie jumped for joy. I winked and told Jamie, "Okay, we're gonna give you some target practice."

"How do you have targets in mind talk?" she asked, her brother crossing his arms in similar curiosity. I pointed at Mark, not far from us, and instructed, "If you're going to use this method, you have to practice talking to people further and further away. Try saying something to Mark."

"He doesn't like us, though," she noted, scrunching her nose up. Trace gave me an expression to say while he wouldn't add to her comment, he agreed. I encouraged, "Then surprise him."

With some reluctance, she closed her eyes and focused. I watched Mark closely, prepared to throw up a barrier if he got caught off guard at the wrong time. But nothing happened. Jamie finally opened her eyes and huffed in frustration, "I can't do it."

"Of course you can," I assured, "Like I said, it takes practice. Like fighting. You won't be good at it immediately."

"Are you good at it?" I shrugged. "I can talk to Mugireti of course, and Mark and I have started to communicate. I'm still having trouble with K.C., though."

"What about Garrett and Will?"

"Actually," Trace butted back in, "I don't think that's how rider telepathy works, Stickers."

"You don't know. C'mon, Jamaica, try it!" Jamie urged, taking my hands and bouncing on her toes. To humor her, I closed my eyes.

Hey Garrett, can you hear me?

"Ha!" Jamie laughed, and my eyes popped open to see Garrett looking around. And when he spotted the three of us, his hands went to his hips with a grin stretching ear to ear.

Squirt, you tryin' to scare the livin' daylights outta me?

My eyes widened. "He answered back."

How did you-? But Jeff- he's never told us about talking outside the cluster.

I figured you'd try any day now. Clusters don't always interact. More times than not, they never meet. But riders are supposed to be able to talk to riders, no matter if they're in the same cluster or not.

"What's he saying?" Jamie whispered. I replied, "Riders can talk to each other even in they're not in the same cluster."

"I thought with riders it was a matter of trust," Trace pointed out. I relayed this to Garrett, who had a simple answer.

Yes. And I assume you trust me enough, seein' as we're talkin'. How's your back?

I gave Trace his answer as Garrett went back to practice with Mr. Maruken. And since I didn't want to distract him too much, I gave a short response.

Raw.

"So, what's next?" Jamie pressed. I told her to keep trying with Mark, and though it didn't completely work, I thought I saw my cousin flinch a couple times. And finally, at the end of practice, Jamie's eyes snapped open in surprise.

This is your doing, isn't it?

I caught the annoyed look on Mark's face as he strode towards us, so I told Jamie to go hang out with Kaia. When Mark reached Trace and me, he accused, "You did this."

"I don't know what you're talking about," Trace shrugged. I could see Mark's patience level drop a few points, so I fessed up, "I'm helping Trace teach Jamie how to use her powers."

"So you set her on me?" he huffed. I excused right back, "She needs practice with distance."

He laid his face in his hand, grumbling, "Well I think *her* practice gave *me* a headache."

"Sorry," I apologized, "Maybe Joey can help you out with some headache medicine."

He nodded and headed toward the workshop, going in just as Will walked out. He smiled at us, but something about it showed that his mind was busy on other things. He walked across the sparring area to Garrett and Mr. Maruken, and a moment later, Trace's dad left to practice with Andrew instead. Trace muttered, "What do you think that's about?"

"Maybe they're just talking," I guessed, though once Garrett made several glances toward me, it became clear that I was wrong. We watched the two curiously, and after another minute, they began to approach us. "Think we're in trouble?"

"Can't imagine why," I thought. The two men stopped in front of us, Will requesting, "Trace, can we speak with Jamaica, please? Alone?"

My boyfriend glanced at me before hesitantly backing away. I asked cautiously, "What's going on?"

"It's about your arm," Will started. I stopped, "Garrett said I'll have to rehabilitate it, I know-"

"Squirt." I quieted for Garrett so Will could continue, "Your arm will scar up like the other, and as long as Joey keeps his eye on it, there should be no problem with infections."

"But?"

He sighed, "But…your left arm is your dominant. It handles a lot more of your finer motor skills, like writing, picking up objects…fighting."

"What does that mean?" I pushed, though I wasn't sure I wanted him to answer. Will rubbed the side of his temple before Garrett finally spat out, "Your arm is damaged, squirt. And it might affect your fightin'."

"What do you mean it'll affect my fighting?!" I looked frantically between them, "You mean I'm not gonna be able to fight anymore?!"

"Now, Jamaica, we didn't say you'd be incapable-"

"But he just said my arm is damaged!" I protested to Will, "If I can't fight, the Emperor- oh my god the Emperor-"

"Jamaica, just calm down-"

"He wanted me to learn my place, that's why he cut me. He knew if I couldn't fight-"

170

"Jamaica." Will set his hands on my shoulders, his gaze easing me down. "All this means is that you'll have to work a little harder to keep your arm mobile. It's a task that takes dedication, determination, and a little bit of stubbornness-"

"-but seein' as how much you're like you mama, that shouldn't be much of a challenge," Garrett encouraged, "and if some angles still pain ya after you've healed, we'll work around it."

I showed my understanding, and then decided, "I'm gonna go home for the day."

"Jamaica, you still have practice with your cousins-"

"Hey, Mugireti, you coming with?" I called to my dragon. He got to his feet, though the ridges above his eyes showed clear confusion.

Don't you still have practice?

"Just like her mama, can't change her mind once she's set," Garrett grumbled. Mugireti joined me just as the trees got thicker, and the sounds of practice began to fade.

Will and Garrett just told me my cut could affect my fighting. I need time to think.

You can't beat yourself up, Jamaica. You can't control what the Emperor does.

Maybe I couldn't control Izoles. But just the same, it felt like there were so many other things that if I had just done something different, I could've avoided the injury.

I don't have the coordination in my right arm like I do my left. Mugireti, what if it doesn't heal like it's supposed to? What if I can never fight again? What if-

Don't finish that sentence.

What if I can't beat the Emperor?

Mugireti stopped and snaked his head around so that I would have to stop too. We were now deep into the woods, almost at the base of my house's hill.

You know what? Unfortunate things will happen along the way, but you are going to get right back up. Izoles has slashed you open twice now, and you survived. Mark accidentally roasted you yesterday, *and you're already back on your feet. No one can deny your resilience. But you want to know what's even more important than that?*

After a moment, I murmured, "What?"

He leaned his face in until he was pressing the top of his head along my body.

You are not expected to make this journey alone. We are all here to help you, protect you, guide you, just as you are for us. And don't think for a second that one bad man is gonna scare us away.

I wrapped my arms around his jaw, whispering, "Thanks, Mugireti. I needed that."

We walked the rest of the way to my house in silence. Mugireti eventually split off to go lay down by the forest edge so he could wait for Pashince. I opened the front door, hiding behind it when Dragon came bounding out. And once she calmed down, I carefully knelt to scratch her belly, careful not to agitate my back too much. And maybe she understood that, because she covered my face with even more slobber than usual.

"Hey, kiddo, home so soon?" Dad said in the doorway. I shrugged, a sort of glum feeling settling in my stomach. My self-esteem was supposed to be boosted by what Mugireti said, wasn't it? So why did I feel so powerless?

"Sweetheart, what is it?" He coaxed, coming out and sitting down beside me. Next thing I knew, I found myself crying and accepting his careful hug. I guess it hadn't hit me just how scary everything was still. Maybe I thought that after a year, I'd gotten used to it. But nothing could stop me as I began to bawl, Dad's comforting words barely registering, and Dragon's licking providing little distraction. What was I supposed to do? Everyone had made it so clear that we were fighting for survival, and if I couldn't fight...

Eventually, Mugireti was curling himself around the three of us, and the sobbing started to hurt my throat. Dad rested his chin on my head, voice quieting.

After probably around ten minutes, I finally managed to calm down a little, so Dad asked, "What's going on, kiddo?"

"Everything," I croaked, feeling Dragon's head and paws on my feet as she lay down. My dad mumbled, "Hang on a sec. I've got an idea."

He got up and went inside, so I curled up and looked down on the town.

Is there anything I can do to help?

Don't leave.

Of course not.

Mugireti curled just a little closer. It seemed like Dad took forever, but he came out with a couple beach towels, a blanket, and couch pillows stuffed into his arms, two plates with sandwiches precariously balanced on his hand. "If I remember correctly, the constellation Leo should be up in the sky tonight. So will Scorpio, and the Ursas- I don't think we'll be able to see Orion tonight, but there are plenty of others we can find."

I did my best to help him lay the towels and blanket out on the grass, setting up the pillows against Mugireti's belly. Dad handed me a plate and sandwich, and my stomach growled. I hadn't realized I was hungry. Just audible enough to hear, I said, "The sun doesn't set for another few hours."

"Then we'll just have to fill the time until then," he smiled, pulling me into a gentle hug. I whispered, "I love you, Dad."

He kissed the top of my head. "I love you too, kiddo."

----0----

A week and a half later, I was back to sparring practice, despite my dad's concern. I ducked under Trace's sword and pushed it away when he made a swing for my waist. The push was sloppy, and I knew it, but that didn't stop me from trying to attack back. I failed miserably, overestimating the ability of my injured limb, paired with my back. With a gasp of pain, I took a knee, tenderly grasping my arm. Trace was next to me in a second, sword discarded in favor of checking on me.

"Jamaica, you've been at this for a solid hour, at least take a break."

"I have to keep pushing it. I need to be able to fight-"

"You *need* to cut yourself some slack- hey!" I took a swipe at him with my dagger, and he easily disarmed me, tossing the wooden weapon out of my reach. "C'mon, please? I know you're trying to get back into it, but if you overwork yourself, you might do more harm than good."

"Fine," I huffed, allowing him to help me up. I blew the hairs strewn in front of my forehead away from my eyes and wiped the sweat off. My boyfriend questioned, "Are you sure you're okay? You look dizzy."

I was feeling a little woozy, and admitted it. "Just take a breather. If you ask me, you don't give yourself enough credit for everything you've done already."

As we walked toward the workshop my adrenaline from practice started to wear off. I muttered, "It's only necessary for my arm."

"Hm," He hummed as he opened the door to the shop. Bruno greeted us, "Hey kids, you alright?"

"We're fine, Bruno," Trace answered as I sat down against the nearest wall. He squatted down next to me. "Jamaica just needs to rest for a little while."

"Do you?" Bruno smiled and folded his arms at Trace's surprise before suggesting, "Head back to practice. I'm sure Jamaica won't need help resting."

Trace squeezed my hand before standing up and walking back outside. Bruno winked at me as he adjusted his smithy gloves and started back towards the other side of the shop. But I piped up, "Bruno? Why do you always wear those gloves?"

He glanced at his hands momentarily, his forearm tensing up. "I work around hot metal, Jamaica. I kind of need them for protection."

"But you never take them off. Not for practice, or meals-"

"Jamaica," he intervened, sharper than I thought he would. His jaw clenched several times, but he finally sighed, "Maybe another time."

"Then-" I caught nervously, "-then can I ask about your dad?"

He turned full around, replying, "Why are you suddenly so curious about me?"

"Well, I have to rest. I don't have anything better to do." It was a dumb excuse, I knew that, and I didn't expect it to work. If anything, I thought it might frustrate him. But though his shoulders were tight, he finally eased himself down to the floorboards in front of me. "What would you like to know?"

I opened my mouth, and he added, "Other than my gloves."

I thought a moment, trying to figure out what to ask first. "You said your father ran the OAD, and it was safer when he did."

"Yes. And I meant that."

"Can you tell me about it? Or him?" He wore a bittersweet smile, resting his elbows on his knees. "I can't say I remember too much. I haven't been there since I was- young. It was a prison outpost, and my father, in his time, was the chief of the facility."

A prison outpost made sense with the setup of the grounds, I guess. "Your father was a police chief?"

"And in a time with extreme prejudice against immigrants, which he was."

My eyes widened. "Really? Where was he from?"

"Both he and my mother were Taiwanese, and like many others, they came to America for the opportunity to start fresh. I can still remember how proud I was that my father ran that outpost. For me, it was the epitome of good triumphing over evil, that he could be in such a high position despite the adversity against him. His officers respected him for the most part, and in my childhood mind, I always imagined the inmates did too."

The smile began to fade. "And even as a little kid, I always wondered if my brother would be thrown in there. Sometimes, I hoped for it."

175

He trailed into his thoughts at that, so I cautiously pushed, "So, then, how did your brother get control of it? The guards- I mean, the officers- they didn't double-cross your father, did they?"

"No," he shook his head, "While it was sad to lose him, my father died of a heart attack when I was six. My family knew he had health issues, and that one could come along any day. It pained my mother too much to take me back to the outpost, and when I ran away, I decided that it reminded me too much of him. My brother, on the other hand, used our father's image for his own use to gain control of the place. To turn it into what it is now."

The young agent Ed crossed my mind, causing me to wonder, "Maybe there are still good people there, then. Maybe the Emperor's blackmailing them, or something."

"I doubt that," he halfheartedly smiled, "My brother's been in control a long time. If there were officers loyal to my father, they're long gone."

"Maybe the ones loyal to him. But what about new ones? Younger blood?" His gaze hard and steady, he mumbled, "If there are younger agents working for him now- and for your sake, we'll say through blackmail- I pity them."

A few seconds of silence passed, and then he asked, "You seem fairly sure that my brother is taking new recruits. Care to tell me why?"

I glanced at him, but my eyes fell to my shoes. Could I really tell him about Ed? Would it even matter to him? "Just a thought, I guess."

Bruno and I didn't talk anymore on the subject after that, though he offered to answer my questions anytime if I had more. My tongue had gone limp after thinking about Ed. He was an agent, sure. But the pure fear and panic Trace and I witnessed when he was scared for his family- that wasn't the kind of fear people could fake, not even in movies. He had to be telling the truth. And if he was, who's to say he was the only one in his predicament? The OAD was a large facility after all. With the swarms of guards I'd seen in my two trips, it had to be possible

176

that some of them, like Ed, were there because they were being threatened by Izoles. But I had a feeling that was something I'd have to prove on my own.

Beginnings

One month later

"Muffin, there's no need to cry," Mom soothed, wrapping her arms around me. I welcomed the hug, but it didn't provide as much comfort as it did before.

"I know you're not really here, but-"

"Jamaica," she cut me off firmly, "I am as here as you need me to be. And I know it's been almost ten years now, but if you ever need me, I will be right here."

She pulled back to tap my temple, and then let go as someone cleared their throat. We both looked over to see Courtney waiting.

"Oh," Mom tried to laugh, "You're waking up. It seems I better go."

I wanted to protest, but I just let her slip away again, disappearing into nothing. But Courtney didn't turn and vanish with her. "You're not actually waking up quite yet. I wanted to talk to you myself. I'm- sorry, that I'm not of more use to you. I'm working on it. And if you need anything, I'll do whatever I can, I just-"

She seemed to stop, seeing my eyes downcast. "…I know that- it's not the same. Not her. I'm just trying to help, and-and I don't know how."

Her voice grew fuzzy as she said, "It looks like you really are waking up now…"

My eyes opened to hear the pitter patter of rain against my window. A small fork of lightning flashed in the distance, and a few seconds later, a soft roll of thunder. I climbed out of bed and snuck into Dad's room. Dragon lifted her head, tail wagging a little, so I put a finger to my lips and whispered, "Shhh."

Why I shushed my dog, I don't know. But she put her head back down and either watched me through the corner of her eye or fell back asleep. I quietly plucked a picture frame from my Dad's dresser, and slipped back out, hoping the crackle of the carpet hadn't awoken him. Once I returned to my room, I sat on the floor, leaning against my bed, and just stared at the picture. Dad looked so elegant and high class in his tux, and yet somehow, still exactly like himself. And Mom…her reddish-brown hair had been done up in a bun with two little strands coiling down in front of her ears and brushing the lace covered skin between her neck and shoulders. Dad recalled that the back of the veil nearly touched her hips, and the train trailed easily a few feet further than the lens could capture that day. But this picture was closer, catching the embroidery details on her dress, and the creases in each of their faces. They had their foreheads pressed together and their fingers intertwined, creating a perfect profile of them.

I hugged the picture to my chest and felt the tears welling, warm and thick. Lightning cracked, and thunder rumbled louder as the center of the storm drew closer. I wanted my mom.

----0----

"Jamaica," someone murmured, "Jamaica, wake up, sweetheart."

I slowly pried an eyelid open to see Dad standing in my doorway. "Happy birthday, kiddo."

A drowsy smile slipped over my face as I moved to get up. Then something fell over into my lap. Realizing it was the picture frame, I tried to pick it up and brush it off as no big deal without Dad seeing it, but he had already walked into the room. Of course he would know the picture, he saw it every day. He lowered himself down until he was on his butt next to me, one hand holding the side of the frame when I offered it back. "I miss her too, Jamaica."

"It's been ten years," I softly mourned. He replied, "I know."

After a moment, he stood up, taking the frame with him. "C'mon, let's not think about it today. Your mom wouldn't want that."

The doorbell rang, followed by Dragon rushing downstairs, her barks echoing through the house. Dad chuckled, "Looks like the party committee's here."

"I thought Mark and K.C. weren't supposed to be here until, like, eleven," I yawned. He smiled, "They're late."

I grabbed for my alarm clock to see that it was almost eleven thirty, and then scrambled up to follow my dad out of the room. As he went to his room to replace the picture, someone knocked on the door.

Are you even awake?

It's almost eleven thirty, Mark, why would I be asleep?

You really want me to answer that?

...No.

"I'll go get it," I sleepily called as I got to the stairway. I clunked down the stairs and opened the door for my cousins, Mark grinning as he did a once over of my pajamas. K.C., meanwhile, gawked, "You're not even dressed?! Girl, we're gonna have to fix this."

I granted her a laugh as they came in, Dad just reaching the base of the stairs. While Mark picked up a box of party supplies he'd set on the porch, K.C. took my wrist and started to lead me towards the second floor. "K.C.-"

"I am fixing what needs to be fixed!" She retorted before Mark could say anything. He grumbled, "Girls."

K.C. pulled me back up to my room and sat me on my bed so she could rummage through my closet. "Why are you looking through my clothes?"

"Because-" she finally turned around, holding my nice white blouse and a pair of dark denim shorts, "-You have amazing clothes and you never wear them, so I will be darned if you don't on today of all days."

"It's just my birthday-"

"Just your birthday? Dude, your fifteen now. And you've got a summer birthday too, which means you get to wear the good clothes." She pushed my own clothes on me and demanded to see. So as I changed out of my pajamas, I humored, "Good clothes?"

"Hey, I don't turn fifteen until November, and you *know* how my mom is. The most I can get away with on my birthday is a knee length skirt and half calf boots with leggings."

"So you're taking your strangled fashion sense and forcing it on me?" I joked, turning for her to see. She nodded, "Absolutely. Now put these on-"

"H-Hey! Where did you get those?!" I snatched the pair of shoes from my cousin's hands. They were a pair of Mom's, admittedly a pair I'd stolen from my parents' closet and never told Dad about. They were Mom's wedding heels, slightly yellowed with age, and when I was little, Mom had promised to let me wear them when I got married someday.

K.C. excused, "What? They were in your closet."

When she saw the expression on my face she complied, "Okay. You don't have to wear them. Is everything alright?"

I sunk to my bed again. "It's been almost ten years without my mom. I just- I miss her."

"Wait, are those-? Oh god, I'm an idiot, Jamaica, I'm sorry-"

181

"It's fine." She took the heels from me and gently replaced them right where she'd found them. "You know what, I doubt Uncle Bernard will mind all that much if you go bare foot. After all, it's a barbeque party. We'll be outside for the most part, anyways."

I let her do her thing, fishtail braiding my hair over my left shoulder and setting a headband behind my ears. And then she stood back, the look on her face certain that something was still missing. Then she snapped her fingers. "Did Uncle Bernard cut down the hydrangea plant yet?"

"No."

"Does he still keep an exact-o knife in that spare drawer in you guys' laundry room?"

"Why?"

"I'll be right back. Don't move."

"K.C., what are you-?" but she escaped out my door and thudded down the stairs. I heard Mark faintly snip, "K.C.-"

"Not now!" she answered. What was she doing? Especially with flowers and an exact-o knife? A minute later, she rushed back in, a newspaper from the recycling also under her arm. "What are you doing?"

"Just wait! You'll see." She plucked the pink cluster apart into its individual blossoms, and began delicately cutting into the stems. I watched intently, trying to figure out what she was up to, to no avail. When she finally brought the newspaper over with flowers perched in a mound on top, I questioned, "Are you going to tell me what's going on in that brain of yours?"

"Telling you won't be as fun as showing you. Now shush." She started sticking them in my braid, fiddling with the stems in the back. It took her a couple minutes, but she finally let me stand up to look in the mirror hanging over my dresser. A trail of little pink hydrangea flowers zigzagged down the braid like lilies on a pond. I carefully flipped the braid over to see that she had threaded the stems through each other to keep the flowers in place. "Whoa, how did you learn to do that?"

"My Nana was a total hippie in the sixties, remember? She taught me how to make daisy chains, so I improvised a little."

"Wait, your mom's mom was a hippie? What happened to your mom then?"

"I don't know," she shrugged, "Guess she liked corporate money more than peace signs. C'mon, we better go help downstairs before Mark has a hissy fit."

"Hey, I want you two to get along today. Birthday wish," I insisted. She groaned, "Ugh. Fine, but only because it's your birthday. And you better tell him the same thing."

"I will," I promised. We walked back down to see Dad and Mark about halfway done with the streamers. My cousin was currently on a chair attaching a streamer to the light hanging down from the middle of the ceiling. Upon seeing us, he rolled his eyes and dramatically announced, "Ladies and gentlemen, the queen has graced us with her presence. Oh and of course, the birthday girl."

"Hey. You be nice," I pointed at him to make sure he knew who I was talking to, "My birthday wish is for you and K.C. to be friendly for the day."

"Fine."

"And I don't want you butting heads with Trace or Jamie, you hear?"

"I hear, I hear, escucho," he dismissed, going back to his task. I looked at K.C., who, to my relief, was looking back with the same confusion. She popped, "Did you just speak Spanish?"

He stopped again and looked at us for a moment. "Uh, yeah. Been thinking about my dad lately…thought maybe I'd learn a little bit. It is part of my heritage after all."

K.C. shrugged and proceeded to grab the bag of party balloons. I stared at Mark another second before smiling to myself and helping her out.

We got the house looking festive enough in about an hour, and while Mark, K.C., and I got the kitchen set to go, Dad fired up the grill. And not a moment too soon. I had just closed the door on Dragon in the laundry room upstairs when a knock rapped against the front door, causing her to bark and whine, pawing at the corner of her imprisonment. K.C. raced to open the front door, and once she did, she called, "Bruno and the guys are here!"

I galloped down the stairs, getting showered in burly hugs and birthday greetings all around. K.C. shouted, "Hey, hey, watch her hair! I worked really hard on that!"

And so, the party started. Within the next hour, my aunts and uncle showed up, and so did Trace, Jamie, and Mr. Maruken. Anna and Kaia made it as well, but Scarlet couldn't get permission from her parents. I couldn't say I was surprised. She'd been fighting with her parents ever since we got back. Sometimes it was over petty things, like forgotten chores, but it was mainly over her discovery of who Izoles really was to her. It was amazing her mother hadn't banned her from practice yet.

Dinner was fun, with countless burgers and hotdogs devoured, while Jeff and Michael almost had a showdown with the ketchup and mustard. Someone finally did the old west whistle music, and they broke into laughter.

But all this fun came to a point at sundown, Dad bringing out a cake with two number candles lit to say fifteen. I thought the sudden momentous singing was a big fuss for it all, but I bashfully smiled, blowing out the candles. Jamie winked, "What'd you wish for?"

"I'm not telling you," I giggled back. Dad cut up the cake, handing me the first piece. While everyone crowded around to get theirs, I slipped inside the house, taking my cake up to the roof. The stars would be out soon enough, so if I was up here long enough, maybe I could stargaze.

"You know, I thought something was off when I got over here," Trace huffed, coming up through the opening in the roof behind me, "but I figured maybe it was just my paranoia. What's up?"

He plopped down next to me, a slice of cake also having accompanied him. I revealed, "It's been almost ten years without my mom."

His smile shrunk into something more somber. For a while, he said nothing. But when he did finally speak, he declared, "I miss my mom too. But if there's any chance of getting yours back, I'm gonna help you however I can. You deserve that much."

He suddenly slipped a long thin box into view. "And since I forgot to say so, happy birthday, Jamaica."

"It's no big deal," I shrugged, but the corner of his mouth perked up, "Well, I think it is."

He motioned the box a little closer, and I took it. As I removed the lid, he excused, "Mugireti helped me out a bit-"

I felt my gasp catch in my throat as I saw the heart shaped charm hanging on a silver chain. It looked like a moonstone. "I-It's beautiful. How did you two-?"

"Well, Mugireti's an earthbender like you, and I had an idea-" He flipped the charm over to show me the back with my name engraved in cursive. "-I-I hope it's not too much."

"No, no, it's amazing," I assured, taking the necklace out and slipping it over my head. I picked the charm up from my chest and turned it over in my hand, letting it rest in the center on my palm. He continued, "I've thought a lot about our conversation, and about where we stand, and I kinda realized…whatever love is supposed to be…I get nervous and happy when your around, but you help me focus, and center myself. It's-It's like a sort of balance, one I've never had with someone before. And I like that feeling. So, whether that's love or not, I'm staying by your side as long as I can."

I dared to lean over and kiss him on the cheek. "I'd say it's close enough. Thank you."

I wished that the stars would come out just a little faster, to turn this into an even more perfect moment. "Having fun, lovebirds?"

I whipped around to see K.C. halfway out of the roof opening, eyebrow raised with a smirk on her face. I fumbled, "How did you-? When did you-? How long have you been there?"

"I followed Trace," she answered, "Nice necklace, by the way. Now would the birthday girl please come back to the party?"

"Brat," I joked. She returned, "Jealous?"

I stuck my tongue out at her before picking up my forgotten plate of cake and climbing back into the house, Trace right behind me. K.C. took my elbow and told Trace we'd be down in a minute. I asked, "Is something wrong?"

"You and Trace told me about Mark's dad," she informed, much more serious than she was two seconds ago, "So, what can you tell me about your mom?"

"W-What?" I stammered. She explained, "Look, we'd all accepted that Mark's dad was gone. So for him to be alive- well, it suddenly makes the possibility of your mom a lot more believable, if you ask me."

My jaw hung open a little before simply humming, "Really?"

She smiled halfheartedly, "I'm sorry I wrote it off. I know how much your mom means to you. And I agree with Trace, if there's anything I can do to help, I will."

She took my hand and encouraged, "C'mon, let's get back to your party."

----0----

"Ah, high school," K.C. breathed in, she, Mark, and I stepping off the bus for the first time, "The prime education establishment said to break kids' spirits for adulthood."

"Well, aren't you optimistic," I snorted. Mark grumbled, "And to think, I'd have been going here for a year already if my parents hadn't put me in kindergarten a year late."

It was the beginning of September, and the beginning of a new section of the K-12 school for the three of us, and for my friends as well, though I had yet to look for them.

"Aw c'mon guys, I'm sure it's not that bad," I laughed.

I wasn't entirely wrong. My classes were easygoing for the first day, and while I kept feeling the need to pull my sleeves further past my wrists, it wasn't terrible meeting new students. Nonetheless, I immediately went searching for my cousins and friends when lunchtime finally rolled around. I didn't care about the rumors of high school cafeteria food, I'd survived junior high's, hadn't I? Besides, I hadn't eaten breakfast, so anything edible sounded good right now.

Without thinking about it, I walked up to the a la carte station and rolled back my sleeves to handle the spaghetti scoop. "Whoa, nice scars, girl. Did the theatre's makeup department do them for you?"

I glanced at the girl next to me. She had blonde highlights in her brown hair, and her pale eyes were surrounded by silver glittery eyeshadow. While I hated to admit it, my first thought of her was that she was a cheerleader. I muttered back, "Um, no, actually. They're real."

"Please, the only way those are real is if you did it to yourself," she leaned in closer to whisper, "They're on the wrong side, by the way."

I gripped my tray and tried to bite my tongue as she passed me in line with a few other girls. But out of nowhere, I suddenly blurted, "You wanna see if they're real? Then take a look."

I stretched the elastic of my left sleeve as I pulled it up to my shoulder, teeth digging into the side of my cheek as the fabric snagged on still healing areas. "I didn't ask for my scars, but I got them. And you know what? I'm proud of them, too."

"Ooh, she's proud of them," the girl taunted to her friends. And then a familiar voice teased back, "At least she's got something to be proud of."

Thank god for Anna. She poked the girl in the shoulder, saying, "All you have is a pitchy soprano voice and a tacky winner's certificate for an eighth-grade singing competition, Alyssa. I wouldn't get so high on my horse if I were you."

"And you think you're better than me?"

"No-"

"Then why are you still talking?" Alyssa said in just about the most obnoxious way possible. Anna held her ground, stating, "Because she is."

Alyssa and her friends suppressed their laughter, Alyssa waving off, "Whatever, she can't even keep from cutting herself-"

A shockwave went off. It wasn't like my full fields, nor was it very strong. But it was focused enough to send Alyssa's tray into her chest, smashing spaghetti sauce and lemonade across her tank top. I winced, "Oops."

She angrily scoffed before strutting off, probably to get me in trouble. Anna wiggled her fingers after the girl's posse, then grabbed my right arm and hissed, "Are you insane?!"

"It was an accident!" I pleaded, rolling my sleeve back down to my elbow. I took my tray to the register and handed the lady my student ID, and afterwards, Anna led me outside to the table where my cousins were sitting. K.C. admired, "So you decided to show off your battle scars, huh?"

"Are you sure you should do that?" Mark worried, picking at a salad. I huffed, "I'm pretty sure it just got a bratty girl to hate me."

"Oh, she's not just bratty," Anna warned, "She's conniving, cruel, and pure evil."

"Uh, no, I think the Emperor owns that last title," K.C. butted in. Mark added, "Would you like to tell us who 'she' is?"

"Alyssa Peterson," Anna grouched, "She won first place in some solo singing competition for eighth graders last year, and ever since then, she thinks she's all that."

"She sounds pleasant," Mark mused, "You sound jealous."

"As if, flame for brains," Anna mocked. K.C. giggled, "I'm gonna have to write that one down."

"What is she doing here, though? I've never seen her before," I commented right before stuffing a forkful of spaghetti in my mouth. Anna clarified, "Unlike us, she's from a K-8. I guess she got zoned here for high school."

We left the subject there as Kaia and Scarlet showed up, Mark's friends Remy and Neville just behind them, and K.C.'s friend Mila soon after. We overcrowded the table, all our side conversations talking over one another, but no one seemed to mind. If anything, it made the first day a little less intimidating having a group of friends around.

"*Jamaica Zwivelle, to the front office, please. Jamaica Zwivelle to the front office.*" We all quieted a moment before Remy excitedly snickered, "Someone's in trouble!"

Mark elbowed him in the side as I got up to leave. I heard Anna muttering profanity under her breath, but no one said a word as I slung my bag over my shoulder and tossed my Styrofoam plate in the trash. My feet felt like cinderblocks as I walked toward the office. My stupid energy bursts had done this, not me. Of course, I couldn't explain that without sounding crazy.

I reluctantly pushed open the door to walk inside, stopping at the front desk. The receptionist acknowledged, "Hello, how can I help you?"

"I, uh, I got called up." I slowly made my way through the office halls until I found the door labelled Clyde Harrison-Principal. I knocked, and heard a muffled old voice call, "Come in."

When I opened the door, I zeroed in on the silver eyeshadow, right after I saw the big saucy stain on her shirt. "Ms. Zwivelle. Please, sit down."

There was a faint accent in his voice, one that tugged at my brain, even though I'd been in his office before. "Now, which one of you would like to start?"

"She shoved my spaghetti into me, what does it look like?!" Alyssa wigged out as I sat down next to her. I defended, "You started it by teasing me for my scars. And it was an accident."

"Ha! This? Was an *accident*?! Yeah, right-"

"Ms. Peterson, please settle down-"

"Settle down?! I'm still wearing my lunch because of her-!"

"Ms. Peterson." The moment Principal Harrison's voice went cool and steady, she shut up. He turned to me and asked,

"Now, Ms. Zwivelle, you said it was an accident. What happened?"

"I was mad about her judging my scars and saying rude things because of them," I admitted, "I didn't mean to-"

My words caught in my throat, so the principal finally dismissed, "Ms. Peterson, why don't you head down to the nurse's office? I'm sure she can find a spare shirt for you."

Alyssa turned her nose up as she left, closing the door harshly. The principal asked, "How is your arm healing?"

"It's getting there," I answered, trying to keep calm, even though I was talking to the man in charge of the school. He dawned a pair of half-moon glasses as he chuckled, "You and your cousins have been quite the rambunctious bunch over the years. Jumping through classroom windows, climbing the back fence- wasn't Katherine the one to implement barricading a teacher out of his classroom to avoid a test?"

I couldn't help the sound that came out of my nose as I tried not to laugh. K.C. did hate her social studies tests. Principal Harrison nodded with a small smile on his face, "Still, I didn't imagine you would end up sitting across from me for misuse of your powers."

"I didn't do it on purpose, it just-" I was suddenly struck dumbfounded. "You-You know?"

He took a picture frame from the side of his desk and set it in the center. "Be more observant, dear. You might see something you overlooked."

When I looked down, it was a picture of a mother, father, and child. The kid couldn't have been more than twelve. But there, plain as day, lay a golden dragon at the family's feet easily blocking the parents' legs from the knee down. "Now. If you are telling me the truth, and what happened truly was out of your control, tell my son to help you get a handle on it. If you end up in my office again for something like this, I will have to take action."

"Y-Yes, Sir." He wrote me a pass and urged me off to my next class. I made sure to roll my sleeves down again.

When classes ended, Scarlet, Kaia, Anna and I hopped the back gate by the playground and dove into the woods. However, I didn't expect Dad to be waiting for us in the workshop. "So, your principal called."

I looked away, trying to stammer out an excuse. My father started to scold, "It's your first day, Jamaica-"

Scarlet interrupted, "I'm surprised Mark didn't get called up, too. He almost set a science teacher on fire!"

"He what?" Anna gaped. I tried to explain, "This girl started teasing my scars, and I accidentally pushed her food into her...with my powers."

Before Dad could try to ground me, I insisted, "It was one of my energy bursts! I was going to ask Garrett and Will today if they could help me work on it-"

Principle Harrison.

Dad caught my arm before I could rush out the door demanding, "Jamaica, we're not done-"

"I have to go find Garrett-"

"You can find him when we're finished talking-"

"What else is there to talk about? I got bullied, Dad, but I'm fine." He sighed and ran his fingers through his hair. I pressed further, "Look, I'm still self-conscious about my arms, and I know you're worried about other kids picking on me. But I stood my ground today, even if it led to my abilities coming out little. I can handle high school, I promise."

"And when you aren't able stand on your own?" he questioned. Anna stepped up immediately to answer, "Then the rest of us are here for her."

I could see though that his question wasn't meant to imply teenage bullies, his mind was on the bigger threat. So, I was blatant. "We're going to defeat Izoles, Dad, I promise. Maybe it won't be soon, but we will."

Dad's brow knit with uncertainty, and after a moment, he let go of my arm and placed his hands on my shoulders. "I have all the faith in the world that you can, Jamaica. But please don't make

191

promises to me that you might not keep. I'll see you back at home."

I watched him leave the workshop, not entirely sure what to do. "Uh, Jamaica?"

Kaia caught my eye. "I'm fine. Go ahead out to practice."

My friends reluctantly listened, grabbing their weapons from a new rack by the door and shuffling out. I found my hand fiddling with the moonstone hanging around my neck as I began to think. It wasn't often that my dad said something that I didn't believe at all. Especially when it concerned whether he supported me or not.

The workshop door swung open again, and Garrett strode in, quickly spotting me. "Hey, squirt, Anna told me to come find you. Everythin' alright?"

"Y-Yeah, just some stuff with my dad." I played with my necklace a little more before asking, "Why didn't you tell us our principal was your father?"

Though caught off guard, a small smile tugged at his mouth. "Well-"

A shot of pain rung through my skull with no warning, enough to make me stumble and fall.

Hello, and goodbye, my young rider.

Ignoring Garrett's voice, I did the only thing I knew I could in the situation.

Mugireti!

I surrendered to his protection, feeling my consciousness slip away from me. Mom's scream was faint and distant.

----0----

"Jamaica! Wake up, damn it!" I took a sudden breath in to see my dad standing over me. I was still laying on the floor, unmoved from where I'd fainted. He stood over me with a scowl, seemingly foreign in the way it brought out the crease lines of his face. "Dad?"

"That's it," he mumbled, crossing his arms before repeating louder, "That's it! You're done with practice. I'm taking you home."

"Wait-" he started to pull me up by the arm. "-but Dad, I'm okay-"

"I have had it with this. This life is too dangerous for you, I won't let you get yourself killed."

"I'm not gonna-" he whipped me around to my terror and screamed, "You're done! You hear me, Jamaica?! Done! Done, done, do-"

This time I actually did wake up, and when I saw a figure hovering over me, I almost instantly burst into tears, fearful that I'd just had an extremely vivid vision. But it was Garrett who leaned in to soothe the bawling. "Hey squirt, you're alright. You're alright."

"Dad was screaming, and-and he grabbed my arm and- he told me I couldn't practice anymore…" the last word sunk into sobs again. My mentor sat down on the cot I'd been moved to in the sleeping quarters, and I immediately accepted the hug. He steadily murmured, "Now c'mon. Your pa wouldn't scream at ya. He might raise his voice, but he'd never scream."

"He wanted to take me from practice," I croaked through the tears. Garrett carefully thought before replying, "Before you came along, Bernard and Anita were the girl meets boy story to the dime. They were more attached at the hip than two frogs on a lily pad. Just as gross too."

He paused, then continued, "But then, they came home with this lil swaddle of chubby baby, and everythin' changed."

He pinched my cheek lightly as he said this, getting a hiccupped snort out of me that quickly turned into a sniffle. "See, that's what happens when ya become a parent. Suddenly, there's this new responsibility on your shoulders, and you gotta take it with what stride ya can. Your parents understood this better than most couples their age, so they took it very seriously. But five years later, it all changed again for your pa. He was suddenly on his own to raise you."

I didn't say anything, playing with my fingers. "He's just as scared as you are, squirt. You're destined to get sucked into the life that took your mama away, and he's afraid he's gonna lose you too. And speakin' as a father, somethin' happenin' to your kids is one a' the greatest fears you ever have."

I was quiet another moment before creaking, "Is that why you think Ed is your son?"

"What?" Garrett's muscles tensed as he looked down at me, so I hesitantly explained, "Ed. The agent that helped Trace and me. Will told us during the trip that you thought he was one of your sons."

I watched his jaw grind and his eyes trail off before he muttered, "So that's his name."

After another moment, he returned his gaze to me and coaxed, "Why don't you stay here a little longer? I'll have your pa come get ya, okay?"

I nodded silently, irrationally worried about what Dad would say when he found out. Garrett left without another word.

Epilogue

"Gentlemen," the Emperor addressed, "If you would so kindly, state your names."

Two of them looked at each other, the one on the left beginning, "Fernando Landicho."

"Edward Hayes."

"Cory Baker." The Emperor paced a little more before noting, "Names. They're quite powerful, aren't they? Especially in today's world. You look up someone's name, and suddenly, you can know everything about them. How else was I to know about your adorable daughter, or your beautiful girlfriend?"

Fernando and Ed respectively broke eye contact. "However, names can be a plague, a sickness that spreads through ranks and causes one's thoughts to cloud."

The two flinched as their boss brought his weapon out and set it on Ed's shoulder, hairs away from his neck. Cory was perfectly still, seemingly apathetic to the situation. The Emperor thought, "It seems you've been afflicted by the name of the young riders' leader. And for someone like you, there is only one cure."

"Please-" The sword ripped cleanly across, Ed collapsing. Blood flowed faster than he could stop it, and Fernando was soon staring in horror at the corpse. He stumbled back when his

195

superior's eyes glanced over him. Cory's gaze had shifted down and away from his partners. "Mortality is a motivator. For all of you now. When he wakes up, the two of you are dismissed. Cory, if you would, stay behind."

"When he…?" Fernando breathed in confusion. Cory muttered, "Look at his wound."

"What? I-I can't-" But the man's eyes drifted anyway, and watched as the skin began to knit itself back together. He watched in amazement as Ed sat up with a sudden inhale, hand immediately feeling his own neck. The blood was still fresh, coating his skin and staining his collar. The Emperor turned back toward him, and he scrambled away. Fernando helped him to his feet, saying, "C'mon. Let's get you over to Matt."

The two left the throne room, allowing Fernando to let out a sigh of relief. Sure, he was still terrified of what he'd just witnessed, and baffled by how his friend could be walking next to him. But they'd both just walked out of the Emperor's throne room with everything still intact. Sort of.

"How did you do that? The wound-"

"It's a long story, but- I'm like Dan. I had an immortal life. Now I don't."

When they reached Matt's work space, Ed received an understandably appalled reaction. Matt quickly wetted a towel to clean the blood off. Fernando insisted, "I don't understand. Why would he kill you if he knew you'd just come back?"

"In genes like his," Matt began, "It is a theory that he has undergone a different kind of evolution than most humans. How this connects to his powers, I do not know."

"It makes for a lucky cop out, that's for sure," Ed sighed, "And if anything, he's probably reminding me of my own mortality. If he kills me again, I'm done. No coming back to life for me."

Fernando could see him trembling, and didn't blame him. The guy had just experienced a trauma that people only rarely knew. He couldn't even imagine how Ed could be feeling, other than scared. Ed suggested, "We should go see the girls."

"Ed, we're basically on probation at this point. We need to follow orders-"

"I need to know that Jen is alright," Ed defended. As Matt wrung out the bloody water from the towel, he informed, "I assume you know she has chronic bronchitis. Her lungs have been calm for several months, but her coughing is beginning to pick up again."

The older man turned to the two, a seasoned look of worry crossing his eyes. "She is getting worse, Edward. And I am afraid there is little I can do here. She needs proper treatment."

"You say that as if I can persuade him to let her go."

"I say that so that you understand she is under a time limit if you cannot free her from this place." Ed's jaw clenched. Fernando bowed his head before mumbling, "Okay. Let's go see the girls."

Just before the two could leave, Ed asked, "Where's your assistant? I haven't seen him around."

Matt swallowed, refusing to make eye contact. "He has been hiding himself away more often, now that he is under James' eye."

That was all the explanation Fernando and Ed needed. The Emperor was cruel to many, but no one more than that poor boy.

They left Matt to his duties, walking to the cell building sitting out the furthest on the cliff. The two men were silent, no words strong, meaningful, or light enough to break the tension. So, Fernando looked out towards the sea, admiring the sunset. It couldn't have been right that something so breathtaking sat in perfect view of this facility. The smell of salt water was almost overwhelming, and for a split second, he was tempted to remain outside. Abigail wouldn't want to see him. It was his fault she was here in the first place, and being the smart little girl she was, he knew she would figure that out. And she'd hate him for it. But he followed Ed and the guard in anyway, brilliant sun replaced by cold white overhead lights. Ed quickly made his way down to the last cell on the right, the guard barely getting the door open before he rushed in, sweeping his girl into his arms.

Jennifer LeBlanc was beautiful. At only twenty-one, her features already commanded an aura much more authoritative then her small stature might imply. With her icy blue eyes, telling anything but the truth was not an option for anyone. Anyone but Ed. He had her locked with one hand on her back, the other against her short strawberry blonde hair. There was a mumbled 'What is that?' before she suddenly jumped back with a stifled cry. "Is that blood?! Oh my god, is that blood?!"

Of course, his collar was stained. "Jen, I'm fine-"

"Don't you lie to me, Edward!" she demanded through her teeth. He sighed, "It is. But I promise, I'm okay."

Fernando glanced past the two at the nine-year-old with smooth black hair asleep at the back of the cell. Little Abigail. Fernando had never questioned his love for his daughter. It was certainly more than her mother had had, having walked out on them when Abigail was still a toddler, disappearing off the face of the earth. But whenever he was around, she was very quiet, answering his questions with a minimal amount of words.

So Fernando stayed outside the cell, watching over her, listening to Ed reassure his girlfriend that everything would be alright. The guy sure was a good liar when he needed to be.

----0----

The Emperor steadily paced, Cory standing nearby. The superior finally stopped, and inquired, "Cory, do you know who Anna is?"

"Should I?" the agent replied. James nodded to himself before denying, "Of course not. I need you to focus on preparing a new tactic for these riders."

"A new tactic, Sir?"

"I believe Ms. Jamaica gains her power and courage from her team, her cousins. But if her source is cut away, that may change."

"I'm sorry, Sir, I'm not quite following."

198

"Split them from her," The Emperor simplified, "Without her cousins, she weakens. Take her cousins away, give her the ultimatum of her life or theirs. She may be much easier to subdue."

"Pardon my tongue, but that seems incredibly dark, threatening a child's life. Are you sure you-?"

"In this world, you kill, or get killed. And Ms. Jamaica needs to learn her place. With her mind running rampant for her mother, she has created the delusion that her mother can be saved, bringing others with her into the belief. It can be used against her, if done properly." The Emperor finally grasped Cory's shoulders. "As my advisor, I trust I can leave this planning to you?"

"Couldn't we just attack now? Why wait another year?" James smiled, amused by Cory's obliviousness. "Dear boy, the girl needs her education. What fun is it to best an opponent if they are not on your level?"

Though it was clear Cory did not fully understand, he only replied, "Yes, Sir."

"You will see, when this is all over. I will once again emerge the champion, ridding this world of one more rider. You are dismissed."

The agent was hesitant, but obediently left. James grinned. It was just another step in the grand scheme of things. His mission would never be over, there would always be more riders. But he would take pleasure in toying with Ms. Jamaica. She would be too resilient otherwise, and therefore, not ready to face him when the time came. He could not allow that. "Enjoy your year, Ms. Jamaica. We will meet again soon."

www.ingramcontent.com/pod-product-compliance
Lightning Source LLC
Chambersburg PA
CBHW070847120626

46556CB00002B/907